STEPBR

MW00412894

A Hawthorne Brothers Novel

Book Two

By Colleen Masters

Also From Colleen Masters:

Stepbrother Bastard (Hawthorne Brothers Book One)
by Colleen Masters
Stepbrother Billionaire by Colleen Masters
Stepbrother Untouchable by Colleen Masters
Damaged In-Law by Colleen Masters
Faster Harder (Take Me... #1) by Colleen Masters
Faster Deeper (Take Me... #2) by Colleen Masters
Faster Longer (Take Me... #3) by Colleen Masters
Faster Hotter (Take Me...#4) by Colleen Masters
*Faster Dirtier (Take Me...#5) (A Team Ferrelli
Novel)* by Colleen Masters

* * *

DEDICATION

To all my beautiful readers.

Join thousands of our readers on the *exclusive Hearts mailing list* to receive FREE copies of our new books!

CLICK HERE TO JOIN NOW

We will never spam you – Feel free to unsubscribe anytime!

Connect with Colleen Masters and other Hearts Collective authors online at:

***http://www.Hearts-Collective.com**, **Facebook**, **Twitter**.*

To keep in touch and for information on new releases!

STEPBROTHER BROKEN

A Hawthorne Brothers Novel

Book Two

* * *

by Colleen Masters

CONTENTS

Prologue

The Bear Trap Bar
Montana, USA

Adrenaline spikes through my already boozy blood as I slam the bathroom door shut behind me. Flattening my back against the flimsy wooden barrier, I turn to face my unexpected companion for the evening. He towers above me in the dimly lit space, his sculpted features rendered all the more intense by the low light. His close cropped chestnut hair, dark stubble, and effortlessly cool bearing caught my eye from the very first second I saw him. But in such tight quarters as these, every enticing aspect of him is amplified tenfold. The sheer pitch of my fascination with him renders me all but speechless as I drink in the sight of him. At last, we're all alone.

He's easily six feet tall, with a balanced, controlled body well-conditioned by a lifetime of athletics and hard physical work. His cut, perfectly shaped muscles are rippling with barely contained desire. And as visceral as this moment is, it's still hard to believe that what he desires is *me*. God knows I've been fantasizing about finding myself alone with him for weeks on end. But now that we're here together, I'm almost overwhelmed by the hugeness of his want. The staggering, powerful presence of him. My breath catches in my throat as he plants his hands hard on the door above my shoulders, caging me in with mere inches of space between us.

"You sure you're up for this?" he growls, his dark green eyes smoldering in the dim light of the bar bathroom.

I draw myself up with a defiant stare, keeping my eyes trained on his face…no matter how overpoweringly gorgeous it is. Reaching around behind my back, I slide the door's heavy bolt into the locked position. The satisfying, metallic click rings out loud and clear in the small room, despite the cacophony of music and voices roaring in the bar proper. It's the last night of classes at the university nearby, where I'm just finishing off my junior year. Thank god I decided to ditch the frat-sponsored school-spirit shit show on campus in favor something a little more exciting. Or rather, *someone* a little more exciting.

"Does that answer your question?" I breathe, all but vibrating with anticipation.

He cocks a perfectly sculpted eyebrow at me, keeping me pinned between his powerful arms.

"Not quite," he laughs, his voice ragged around the edges, "Try again."

"Wh-what?" I stammer, trying to keep up. At 21, I'm hardly inexperienced with the opposite sex. But even though this guy only has a few years on me, he's making the other men I've been with look like little boys. It's been a long time since I haven't been the more dominant partner in the bedroom…or, uh…*bathroom*, as it were. But where this particular man is concerned, I hardly mind. In fact, I actually find myself wanting to let him take the lead. And that is abso*lute*ly a first.

"I need a yes or no," he goes on, easing his perfectly balanced body toward me. "It's a simple question, Sophie."

My very cells are screaming to feel him against me. If he would just come a *little* closer…

"Would I have come back tonight if I didn't want this?" I point out, resisting the urge to throw myself into his thickly muscled arms.

"To be honest," he murmurs, eyes flicking down to my almost-quivering lips, "I'm having trouble getting a read on you. And let me tell you, that's not something I'm used to. You're gonna have to tell me outright what it is you want, here."

"Why don't you let me show you instead?" I shoot back, letting my hands trail down his rock-hard chest.

"Come on," he says, his full lips spreading into a rakish grin. "You already put it into writing, didn't you? What did that note of yours say again?"

"You're such an asshole," I mutter breathlessly, trying to fight the blush that rises in my cheeks.

"Oh, that's right…" he goes on, letting his torso brush deliciously against mine. He leans in close, his breath warm against my neck. Those firm lips brush against the shell of my ear, sending a shiver down my spine. "You want me to 'Nail you to the wall and fuck you dirty'. Wasn't that it?"

"That…Uh…That was the gist of it," I gasp, my thighs clenching together as a thundering rush of need courses through me.

"Say it then," he demands, brushing a lock of caramel blonde hair away from my face, "Tell me what it is you want."

"I…I just…" I sputter, lowering my gold-flecked blue eyes.

"You'll tell me, won't you," he says firmly. It's not a question.

I force a deep breath into my lungs, gathering up every bit of courage at my disposal (liquid or otherwise). I'm not usually one for nerves, having conquered my stage fright at the ripe old age of four. Usually, that steadiness carries over into my romantic life…but not now. Not with him. For the first time, I don't feel like I'm *performing* desire, I'm *experiencing* it. Turns out, there's a pretty big difference—a difference so big that it almost frightens me. But if I've learned one thing from my life as a performer, it's that sometimes you've got to follow the fear if you want to find the truth.

"Luke," I start softly, my voice low in my chest and husky with lust.

"Yes?" he replies, his smoldering green eyes hard on my face.

I take his face in my hands, my fingers resting against his scruffy, razor sharp jaw, and lock my gaze onto his.

"I want you to nail me to the wall," I whisper, "And fuck me dirty."

A blaze of fiery need erupts in his emerald gaze as he takes me in. For just a second, he looks genuinely amazed that I've risen to the moment. I may have never had a man like him before, but maybe he's never had a woman like me either.

I let my lips part, a snarky jab at the ready to defuse the achingly intense moment. But before I can utter another syllable, he's pinned me to the wooden door with his powerful, tapered hips. A gasp escapes my throat as he snatches my hands from his face and holds my wrists firmly above my head. My entire body lights up like a flare as he brings his mouth to mine, kissing me hard and fast as he presses his incredible form against me.

My back arches as I open my mouth eagerly to his, letting his tongue sweep against mine. Our mouths move together, hungry and searching. I'm stretched out tautly before him, and he explores my dancer's figure with his firm free hand. My nipples go hard as he runs a hand slowly down my side, memorizing the lithe shape of me. He grins as he brushes a thumb over one of those erect peaks, pleased at how quickly he's turned me on.

"How long have you been waiting for this?" he growls, freeing my wrists as he kisses down along my throat. His lips leave sparks of sensation in their wake as they trail along my skin, and it's all I can do to keep putting one word in front of another.

"How long? Oh…Only since your very first class," I laugh breathlessly, writhing under his intoxicating touch.

"Hmm," he replies, grabbing me firmly by waist, "I've never met someone who was so turned on by economic theory. Kinda kinky…"

"It wasn't so much the subject matter as it was the person delivering it," I smile, trying to catch my breath.

"That's good to know," he grins back, his voice straining with need, "It'd be a real shame if you just wanted me for my brain. The rest of me wants in on the action, too."

He shifts his hips ever-so-slightly, and I feel the hard, unbelievable length of him press firmly against my thigh. My eyes go wide as I stare up at him, amazed by the enormity of his need for me.

"Yeah…I think I get it," I breathe, letting my hands slide down his cut torso, "Though I have to say, I wouldn't mind getter a slightly better handle on it…"

"Well Ms. Porter," he grins, as I whip open the buckle of his belt, "I'd be more than happy to give you one last lesson."

The din of the bar is entirely drowned out by the frantic pounding of my heart as Luke slips his hands up under my crop top.

"Go ahead, Prof," I whisper, "I'm a fast learner."

"My favorite kind," he growls back, as I slide my hand down the front of his blue jeans.

So consumed are we by our impromptu study session that we don't even notice as someone starts pounding on the bathroom door. We've got a lot of material to get through, after all. And I have the feeling that I've just discovered my new favorite subject: Lukas Hawthorne.

Chapter One

Sheridan University

Montana, USA

The Day Before...

I roll up onto the balls of my bare feet, perched on the edge of the playing space. Across the stage stands my dance partner, Danny—a quintessential all-American boy. He's got wheat blonde hair, a toothpaste ad smile, and an ego so big he'll have to check it when he flies off to New York City and becomes an instant Broadway sensation someday. I'm allowed to say as much, as one of his closest friends—and because he'd be the first to tell you the exact same thing. We've been rehearsing like crazy people these past few weeks, working to perfect our final dance performance piece of the year. This is our last rehearsal before we show it to our classmates and teachers tomorrow, and our movement teacher Gary has agreed to watch and offer feedback.

Gary, a somewhat fluffy fifty-something man with wispy gray hair, watches from the audience as Danny and I face off across the proscenium stage. He's a tough cookie, our teacher, and isn't one to mince words. I've learned so much from him in the three years that he's been my movement teacher; but above all, I've learned to cultivate an alligator-thick skin. And as someone who plans to pursue a career in the performing arts, that's about the most valuable thing I could ever attain.

The song "Lebanese Blonde" by Thievery Corporation starts playing over the auditorium's sound system, and our dance piece begins. I let my rational mind go quiet as my body moves into the space. Danny and I advance toward each other as the song's trippy, abstract introduction goes on. Our choreography was carefully crafted to strike a balance between the styles of modern and jazz, but I'm not thinking about all that now. I'm not thinking about anything.

I'm simply moving.

Danny and I meet at center stage, mirroring each other's movements precisely as we mark time with the music. As I roll my body around to face the audience, I catch a glimpse of Gary's face. It's pulled into an exasperated scowl. I stumble to a halt as my teacher waves his hand dismissively, signaling our resident sound technician to cut the music. He does, and Danny straightens up with a start.

"Is something wrong with the track?" my friend murmurs in my ear.

"No," I tell him, "I think something's wrong with *us*."

"Impossible," Danny scoffs, "We were flawless. Obviously."

"I think Gary may have a slightly different opinion," I reply, plastering a phony smile onto my face as our teacher appraises us.

My friend and I stand side-by-side in front of our teacher. My long blonde hair is arranged in a loose braid that hangs down my back, and my body is clad in a tight black body suit. My full breasts and ass swell beneath the black fabric, held up by thin straps that crisscross my toned back. I'm no gym rat, but years of dance and yoga (plus the metabolism of a rabbit) have landed me in pretty great shape. Though it doesn't seem to be my figure that has Gary looking so aggrieved.

"Can one of you please tell me what the assignment was for this piece?" he asks in his slightly nasal voice.

Danny and I exchange a quick glance, each daring the other to speak first.

"We were supposed to choreograph a dance piece," Danny starts, "In the tradition of—"

"What *kind* of dance piece, specifically?" Gary presses.

"A…good one?" Danny offers vaguely.

"Good lord…" Gary mutters.

"A *partnered* dance piece," I venture.

Gary gives me a good old slow clap, and I feel the heat rising in my cheeks. I was expecting this performance to go perfectly. More than anything, I wanted to end this year on a positive note. But it looks like my teacher has other ideas.

"A partnered dance piece. Very good, Sophie," Gary says, "So then tell me…If this was supposed to be a dance between partners, why were you following your own lead the entire time?"

I clench my teeth to keep my jaw from falling open.

"I wasn't… I didn't—" I stammer.

"You were, and you did," Gary cuts in. "I could see Danny trying to engage with you, but you were off in your own little world the whole time. It was completely distracting. If anything, Danny should have been taking the lead."

"Because I'm the better dancer, you mean?" Danny asks hopefully.

"Because you're the man," Gary says.

"That's even worse," I mutter, before I can stop myself.

"Not this again Sophie," Gary groans, resting his head in his hand.

"What?" I reply, unable to keep my voice from getting heated, "I'm not allowed to take issue with the totally outdated practice of a male dance partner leading at all costs? It's 2015, for Christ's sake—"

"I am trying to prepare you for a life in the arts, Sophie," Gary cuts me off, "A life that will, if you're lucky, include getting paid to perform. If you want to be out of a job because you can't follow traditional dance protocol without getting a hive of bees in your bonnet, be my guest."

"Maybe I'm not interested in tradition," I reply, folding my arms.

"Fine," Gary huffs, "Screw tradition, if you must. But I didn't stop your performance just now because you weren't letting the man lead. I stopped your performance because you still haven't figured out how to work with a partner at *all*."

I suddenly find myself without any snappy comebacks to dispense. He's got me there. Since arriving at Sheridan University to study dance and drama, collaboration has been my Achilles heel. My work has improved by leaps and bounds when I'm working solo. I can deliver a monologue, belt out a tune, or dance a solo piece with the best of them. But when it comes to working with a partner, listening to someone else…I fall short every time.

"Sophie, you know I love you," Gary goes on, hoisting himself onto the stage and taking my hands gently in his, "I know why trusting people, letting yourself care about people, is so hard for you. But it is something you're going to have to deal with if you want to be a truly great performer."

Sudden tears well up in my eyes as my teacher zeroes in on what's really been holding me back. Just before I started college here at Sheridan, my family was dealt a huge blow. My father Archie was killed in a car crash with a drunk driver back in our home state of Vermont. The loss devastated my family, rendering my mother, Robin, nearly catatonic with grief. My older sister, Madeleine, was already off at college in Washington, and my younger sister, Annabel, was back at home with my mom. I was on my own for the first time in my life, just when I most needed support.

Mere months after the accident, I found myself arriving here at school for freshman orientation. I was closed off, hostile, and so, *so* angry. I've spent the past three years tearing down those defenses, working through my grief in my acting, voice, and movement classes. My classmates and professors have helped me more than I could ever have imagined possible. That's why it's so goddamn frustrating to run up against my same old habits after all this time, to be called out on a difficulty that I want to put behind me. Really, what I want is for the wound of my father's passing to heal. But of course, it's not the sort of thing you can wish away. If I live to be one hundred, not a day will go by when I don't feel his absence.

If only my baggage didn't come crashing down on others quite so often.

"I'm sorry Danny," I say to my friend, swallowing down my tears.

"It's fine Soph," he says, laying a hand on my back.

"You can't rush progress, Sophie," Gary says, "I know you'll find a way around this stumbling block. You just need to give yourself some time."

"Summer classes start in a few weeks… Do you think that'll be time enough?" I laugh, trying to lighten the mood.

"You're incorrigible," Gary sighs, "But hard-headed stubbornness aside, I'm glad you'll be doing the summer session this year. There are some excellent people coming in from New York—they may be able to offer you a fresh perspective. Since I, apparently, am far too *traditional*…"

"You know I didn't mean it like that," I laugh as Gary pulls a melodramatic face.

"As the youths say, 'whatevs'," he shoots back flippantly, hopping off the stage with more agility than seems possible, given his paunch. "On that note, enjoy your summer. See you urchins in the fall."

"What a charmer," I mutter, as Gary takes his leave of us.

"That's one word for it," Danny replies, shaking his head. "I can't believe he cut us off like that."

"Let me buy you a drink to make up for it," I suggest, grabbing my bag from backstage.

"It's not even noon yet," Danny points out.

"One word: Mimosas," I smile, shrugging into my backpack. "Acceptable at any time of the day. Or morning."

"Don't you have class or something?" Danny asks.

"Not for another hour," I reply, "Plenty of time for a good whistle-wetting."

"You've got a problem," Danny laughs, shaking his head.

"Come on," I smile, lacing my arm through his, "Day drinking is what college is for. If not now, then when?"

"That's funny," he says, letting me drag him toward the exit, "I thought college was for building a practical skill set and—"

"Danny. We're in *drama* school," I remind him, "Practicality has nothing to do with it."

"Fair point," he relents, "Lead on, Sophie. Isn't that kind of your thing?"

"Dickhead," I mutter, giving my friend a playful shove as we set off for our favorite taqueria. Nothing like pre-gaming an economics lecture, am I right?

One hour and two drinks later, Danny and I have eased the sting of our botched final rehearsal with a visit to

Pequeño, home of the best tacos (and tequila) in town. We'll have another shot at performing tomorrow, anyway. No harm, no foul. I was lucky enough to be spared the competitive perfectionist gene that my older sister Maddie most certainly inherited. It's a good thing, too—you can't afford to be too precious about rejection when you're trying to be an actor.

"So is your class this afternoon the one with Professor Sexy Pants?" Danny asks, polishing off the last sip of his drink.

"It is indeed," I grin, "I have to say, I never thought I'd actually enjoy one of my general education courses so much."

"Well, it doesn't sound like it's the class you're enjoying, so much as the eye candy," Danny points out, "You couldn't stand going to lectures when that crusty old dude was giving them."

"Thank god for jury duty," I laugh, stretching my arms up over my head. "Having Sexy Pants come in to sub was the best thing that could have happened to my semester."

"Does Sexy Pants have a name, or do his parents just have a sick sense of humor?" Danny asks, lounging back in his chair.

"I believe it's Luke," I reply, "Lukas Hawthorne."

"Professor Hawthorne," Danny repeats with relish, "*Super* hot."

"You don't have to tell me," I laugh, "I can't hear a word he's saying about personal finances, I'm too busy staring at that tight ass of his."

"That's why I'm surprised you're skipping class today. I would have thought that you'd want to take one last gander before the semester is over," Danny says.

"I'm not skipping class," I reply, sitting up straight in my chair.

"Uh, yeah. You are, as of now," Danny says, holding up his cell to show me the time. It's 1:00p.m. The appointed hour of my last economics lecture of the year.

"Shit!" I cry, jumping to my feet and snatching up my backpack, "I've got to go!"

"I'll just put these on your tab," Danny replies, nodding at our empty glasses.

I dig a couple twenties out of my purse, chuck them in my snarky friend's direction, and take off like a shot out the door. The lecture hall is all the way across campus. Good thing I've already got my sneakers on. I race across the grassy lawns that sprawl between the buildings of Sheridan University, dodging picnic blankets, study sessions, and more than a few Frisbee games. Everyone is out and about, celebrating the end of the semester. But not me. Hell, I'll be back here in no time to take some summer performance courses so I have the option of graduating early next year. Besides, I've never been one for school spirit, so the festivities are rather lost on me.

Panting, sweaty, and a little tipsy, I finally lunge into the economics building and wrench open the lecture hall door. A hundred people swivel around in their arena-style seats to face me as I step through the doorway, still wearing my skintight dance clothes. I know they say first impressions are the most important, but this last impression might do a number on my classmates' opinion of me, too. Of course, it isn't really my peers I'm concerned with just now.

"Nice of you to join us, Ms. Porter," says the tall, cut figure facing the whiteboard at the front of the room. When that figure turns to face me, I have to brace myself against the doorway to keep from tumbling down the stairs that lead to him.

Lukas Hawthorne stands there in all his glory, as enticing as he was the first day he showed up to take over our economics lecture. He's about six two, with a broad but balanced body. He wears his chestnut brown hair cut short, and sports the tiniest hint of dark stubble on his distinct jaw. His muscles have been honed by years of training for just about every sport there is. I know, because he did that training right here at Sheridan. He's a legendary athlete around here, particularly in track. His gorgeous face is plastered all over the marketing materials for the school. Those dark greens eyes of his probably convince more people to enroll here every year than the course offerings.

And right now, those eyes are trained on me—looking like a proper hot mess.

"Sorry I'm late," I breathe, transfixed by Luke's steady gaze.

"Don't worry about it," he replies coolly, giving me a searing once-over, "I hear that Jazzercise classes tend to run over now and then."

Stifled laughter rings out through the lecture hall as I glance down at my dance attire. No choice but to own it, I guess. Tossing my messy braid over one shoulder, I straighten my spine and shoot Luke an easy smile.

"Yeah, well. It's a lifestyle," I say, walking confidently to the last empty chair in the room and sinking down with a satisfied smile.

But Luke takes no notice of my slick response. He's already turned away from me and resumed his lesson, as if I'd never appeared in the first place. I let the smile fade from my lips as he goes on. I have to admit, I'm disappointed in his disinterest. Since he first showed up a weeks ago, I've been doing everything in my power to catch his eye. But no matter what I do, I can't seem to snag his interest. I'm not saying that I'm man bait or anything, but I've found that guys are typically responsive when I give them an opening. Not Luke Hawthorne, though. He's barely spared me a passing glance.

Oh well. At least that gives me more time to stare unabashedly at him.

From what I've been able to glean from campus gossip, Luke is back at Sheridan completing his MBA after attending undergrad here a few years ago. He's not an official employee of the school, he just stepped in to teach this class as a personal favor to an old professor. He's a Montana native, a beast on the track, and apparently brilliant.

And naturally, he's a *total* womanizer.

Every other week, he can be seen around campus with a new main squeeze. I swear, there must be a waiting list or something—he turns ladies over like clockwork. But to be perfectly honest, it doesn't bother me one bit that he's an expiration-dater. I've always preferred short, sexy flings to long, dull relationships myself. Especially since my dad passed away, the last thing I want is to be with a guy who insists on getting all emotionally invested from the get go. Give me a passionate tryst over commitment any day.

So consumed am I by thoughts of Luke Hawthorne's romantic preferences that the lecture flies by. In no time at all, the students around me are gathering their things and chatting about their plans for the weekend. This place is going to be nuts starting tonight, it being the last day of the year and all. Keg stands, streaking, and drunken frat bros will be the name of the game around here. For my part, I'd just as soon skip it. My body is only 21, but I think my soul is somewhere in its mid-30's and completely over its binge-drinking college days, thanks.

"Sophia," I hear that familiar, rich baritone say from the front of the room. I turn to see Luke Hawthorne waving me down toward him as the class disperses. "Would you stay behind for a minute? There's something I want to discuss with you."

My stomach does its best washing machine impression as I freeze in my tracks. What could Luke Hawthorne possibly have to discuss with me? My imagination runs wild as my classmates file out around me, stealing curious glances as I make my way toward Luke. Does he want to discuss the seven digits of my phone number? Or where we should meet up for a drink later? Or how he'd like to see me bent over his desk while he—

"What's up?" I ask him, straining to make my voice sound even remotely casual.

He leaves me hanging until the lecture hall door has closed behind the last student. Finally, it's just us. I can feel my pulse quickening with every second we're alone. I've been fantasizing about this for weeks, but I'd given up hope of it ever happening for real. But now that this smart, sexy, unattainable man is standing just a couple of feet away from me, I'd say things are getting very real, very fast.

"I was hoping to catch you alone before you left for the summer," Luke tells me, crossing his thick, muscular arms. The sleeves of his tasteful button-down are rolled up to above his elbows, and tighten around his sculpted biceps. I have to prompt myself to respond.

"Oh. Uh. Why is that?" I ask him, looping my thumbs through the straps of my backpack, "Am I in trouble or something?"

"Not yet," he says, the corner of his mouth lifting into a knowing smile.

Holycrapholycrapholycrap, I think excitedly to myself, *Is he seriously about to go all dirty professor on me? How did I get to be so lucky? Should I have brought an apple or something?*

"But you might be, if you don't course correct. And soon," he goes on perplexingly.

My brow furrows as I look up at him from my measly height of five six.

"Sorry, I'm not sure what you're talking about, Prof," I laugh lightly.

"I'm talking about the effort you put into this class, Ms. Porter," he says bluntly, "Or rather, the lack of it."

My half smile fades away as I realize this meeting is going to be a lot less sexy than I'd hoped.

"With all due respect," I say, drawing myself up under his condescending gaze, "Econ. 101 wasn't exactly my priority this semester. I didn't have a lot of effort to spare."

"Yeah, that was pretty clear," he shoots back, cocking an eyebrow at me. "You barely turned in any of your assignments, you were late more often than not, and I'm not convinced you've to listened to a word I've said these past few weeks."

That's because I was too busy checking out that fine ass of yours, I think, face reddening with embarrassment. I don't mind being called out on failing at something I care about deeply. But being scolded for not putting effort into something totally irrelevant to me really grates.

"Look. Luke. Can I call you Luke?" I ask, cutting the bullshit.

"By all means," he replies, looking amused.

"I honestly couldn't give less of a shit about this class," I tell him, "I'm just here to fulfill my graduation requirements. I'm a performer. That's what matters to me. That's what I spend my every waking hour trying to get better at."

"I understand being passionate about your hobbies," Luke cuts in, "But it's important to—"

"Performing isn't a hobby," I snap, "It's what I plan to do for the rest of my life."

"That's what I used to think about sports, too," Luke replies condescendingly.

"Well, that's a totally different story. No one really gets to be a professional athlete," I say, crossing my arms.

"No one really gets to be a professional actor either," he shoots back, "It doesn't sound that different to me, Sophie."

I stare up at Luke, my jaw clenched tightly. In about three minutes, this man has shattered my esteem of him into a thousand pieces. I should have known that someone like him would turn out to be a total asshole. No one man could be as gorgeous and brilliant as he is and still be a good person. That must be a law of physics or something.

"I'm sure you're not used to hearing this, Luke," I say, all joking aside, "But you have no idea what the fuck you're talking about."

"There's no need to get upset," he tells me, "I thought you could use a bit of honesty from someone at this school. It's a shame to see someone as bright as you waste her potential."

"Let me guess. You think I should abandon my dreams, sell out, and become an upstanding citizen like you?" I shoot back with a laugh. "Thanks, but I'll pass."

"We'll see," he shrugs.

"Yes. We will," I say resolutely, turning on my heel, "Enjoy the rat race, Prof."

I storm out of the lecture hall, leaving Luke Hawthorne behind in the dust. My hands are shaking with indignation. This guy doesn't know the first thing about what I do. What could a MBA-toting jock know about art, or expression, or inspiration? I can't tell if I'm more outraged by his assumptions or disappointed that he's just another macho asshole. As an assertive woman, I'm used to men trying to tear me down to make themselves feel more important. It was ridiculous of me to imagine that this guy would be any different.

As I burst back into the warm afternoon, I swallow a huge gulp of fresh air and do my best to calm down. This guy's opinion of me doesn't matter. I'll never see him again in my life. I should just shake off his criticism and look forward to a summer full of classes that won't include a single money-minded asshole.

But for some reason, Luke's words cling to me like a wool sweater in this summer heat. It wasn't just criticism he had for me, after all, but praise. He thinks I'm bright. He thinks I have potential...*and* he thinks I'm wasting it. Well, add him to the list of people I'll be proving wrong once I carve out the life I want for myself, no matter what it takes. God knows, there are already enough names on that list...what's one more?

Chapter Two

I'll say this for Luke Hawthorne: he certainly
motivates me to bring my a-game to the final day of
performances for the year. My fellow drama students and I
spend the day presenting our final scenes, songs, and
movement pieces for each other and our professors. Danny
and I are scheduled to perform our dance piece at the very
end of the day, and I can barely contain my excitement.
When we get out on that stage again, it's like we're
entirely different performers than we were the day before.
Our bodies are entirely attuned, our every movement
energized with a determination I haven't felt since first
arriving at school. We leave everything on the stage,
losing ourselves in our last performance of the year. And
our hard work doesn't go unnoticed this time.

"Good goddamn," Gary gasps, wrapping us up in a
bear hug as applause rains down from our peers and
teachers, "I don't know what the hell happened to you two
overnight, but I suggest you nail it down and keep it
forever!"

I can't help but laugh at the idea of keeping Luke
Hawthorne nailed down forever. If such a thing is even
possible, I'll happily leave the task to some other poor sap,
thank you very much.

Elated by our job well done, Danny and I walk on air
as we leave the performing arts building at dusk. We walk
across campus with our arms thrown around each other,
taking in the gorgeous night. I notice more than a few
women—and men—stealing glances at Danny as we make
our way past. I can't blame them for starting. My friend is
Hollywood-handsome and stylish as hell. But even though
we have great chemistry as performers, Danny and I have
never once hooked up here at Sheridan. He's bisexual, and

I'm pretty sure every single one of our fellow drama students harbors a crush on him. But our friendship has always outranked any sexual tension that might crop up between us—and I'm glad, too. I'm not very good at keeping my romantic interests around for more than a couple of weeks, and Danny is someone I want to have in my life for many years to come.

"So, what do you think for tonight?" he asks me now, his arm thrown over my shoulders, "Every single frat is throwing some kind of party. Would you prefer togas or a tiki party? I'm pretty sure both will manage to be offensive, but—"

"Ugh. I don't want to ruin this day with a crappy frat party," I groan, "You hate those things as much as I do. Why bother?"

"Do you have a better idea?" Danny asks, "We could go watch shitty Disney movies with the drama freshmen, if that's more your speed."

"Why don't we go somewhere off campus?" I suggest.

"Off campus?" Danny gasps theatrically, "What a novel idea!"

"I *know*. But believe it or not, there's an entire world outside of Sheridan," I reply, "Why don't we explore it a bit?"

"Do you know a place?" he asks.

"Not really," I shrug, "But I'm sure we can find something. Come on. Be a grownup with me!"

"All right, fine," Danny sighs, "But if we accidentally end up in a serial killer's basement or a furry convention or something, it's on you."

"I can live with that," I assure him, "Nothing could be worse than another undergrad party."

Danny and I part ways to go change for our big night out, each of us heading off to our own dorm rooms. If our school had co-ed dorms, we'd definitely be roommates by now. But I guess that'll have to wait until we're living the dream in New York City together. And by "dream" I mean sharing a tiny shoebox apartment, working four restaurant jobs each, and maybe getting to audition for something once a month, of course.

My actual roommate, a very quiet bio major named Kim, doesn't seem to be home—which means I get to blast my music as I get ready for tonight. I plop down in front of my laptop and put on some MGMT, singing along as I give my social media pages and email a cursory once-over. Just as I'm about to close my laptop and get dressed, a new message pops up in my inbox. It's from an address I've never seen before, and the subject line simply reads: "Re: Our Conversation". I click on the email absentmindedly and begin to read…

Hey Sophie,

I wanted to follow up with you after our conversation yesterday afternoon. It wasn't my intention to discourage you. I do think that you're a very promising student, but I also feel that it's my responsibility as your teacher to hold you to the standard of excellence, I'm sure you can meet if you put your mind to it. I know that your heart is set on performing at this point in your life, but I urge you to keep an open mind. Based on the assignments that you actually turned in for my class, and your contributions to our classroom discussions (however rare they may have been), I can tell you have a sharp, entrepreneurial intellect. Don't let it go to waste.

Best,
Lukas Hawthorne

I sit back in my desk chair, fuming as I stare at Luke's message. How can one person be so simultaneously aggravating *and* encouraging? So condescending while voicing a vote of confidence? One thing is for sure. I don't have the time to parse Luke's intentions for writing this little note before happy hour is over. Instead of replying to my esteemed professor, I forward his note to Danny, including a few thoughts of my own:

Can you believe this prick? I may have spent every one of his lectures fantasizing about him nailing me to the wall and fucking me dirty, but this is too much. Someone needs to finally leave Sheridan and get his ass handed to him in the real world before doling out life advice, am I right?

Satisfied with my retort, I crank the music up even louder and get down to business. It isn't often I get excited about going out around here, but I have a feeling tonight's going to be one for the books. And I, for one, intend to look awesome for it.

***

"Here it is," I breathe, grabbing Danny's arm as our cab rolls to a stop.
"Are you kidding me?" he says flatly, squinting through the car window.
"What? So it's a little edgier than the places we usually go…"

"A butter knife is edgy," Danny hisses, "This place looks fucking dangerous."

Our cab is idling in front of a long, low building, with a rough-hewn wooden exterior and corrugated tin roof. A sign above the door proudly proclaims that the establishment is called The Bear Trap. A quick internet search of nearby dive bars led Danny and I to its door, though one of us seems far more enthusiastic about this little plan now that we're here.

"I'm sure it'll be fine," I assure Danny, handing the cab driver his money and stepping out onto the curb.

"Maybe for you," he mopes, standing beside me as the car pulls away. "You're a smoking hot babe. I get the feeling that this place may not be as hospitable to pretty boys like myself."

"Then you'll just have to stick with me, won't you?" I smile, lacing my fingers encouragingly though Danny's.

His outfit for tonight does skew a little more glam than usual, though mine is more in the grungy direction. While Danny rocks his black skinny jeans, I've chosen a vibrant red miniskirt and white crop top for tonight's festivities. My caramel blonde hair hangs long and tousled down my bare back, and I've got my best pair of black stilettos on to boot. I've spent of my time at drama school wearing nothing but leggings and tee shirts, so any excuse to dress up a little is one I'll gladly take.

"We can stay for a couple rounds, max," Danny relents, turning toward The Bear Trap, "But then it's back to our safe little Sheridan bubble, OK?"

"How the hell are you going to survive New York if you can't even handle a little Montana dive bar for one night?" I laugh.

"Are you kidding? I'll be among my people in New York," Danny replies, "It's the good old country boys that worry me."

"Relax," I tell him, heading for the door, "Everything's gonna be just fine."

A wall of sound slams into us as I wrench open The Bear Trap's door. For a moment, I'm almost too stunned to take another step. The bar is full of rowdy locals, clustered around scuffed tables and along the long wooden bar. Hard country rock blares over the sound system, and the crowd is a sea of denim and leather. The men sport baseball caps and bulging muscles, the women rock tight jeans and bottle blonde hair. Danny rolls his eyes as he surveys the patrons.

"Well, at least there's enough leather for my taste," he remarks flatly.

"A bar's a bar, right?" I yell back over the rollicking music, "Let's make like the locals and pound a few back."

"I'm gonna need more than a few to get over this music," Danny replies, making for the bar.

"What? You don't like country?" I grin.

"I'm not even going to dignify that with a response," he glares back at me.

We sidle up to the bar, squeezing between the sardined bodies of regular customers. I catch the bartender's eye first and call out our order for two gin and tonics. The bartender looks at me a little skeptically—I get the feeling this is more of a PBR and whiskey joint—but furnishes us with our first round all the same. With my cold cocktail in hand, I finally feel like I can relax and get a feel for this place. Two barstools open up, and I settle into one beside Danny. Sipping my drink, I turn to give The Bear Trap (and its male patrons) a little once over.

My eyes sweep over most of the guys here without pause. Trucker hats and bad mustaches are both deal breakers for me, alas. But as I lean around Danny to check out the other end of the bar, my gaze comes to a screeching halt as it alights on a very familiar face. A face

I'd never expect to see in a place like this. The sculpted, arresting face of one, Luke Hawthorne.

"What the hell?!" I breathe, hiding behind Danny at once.

"What? What's the matter?" my friend asks, baffled by my behavior.

"Don't look," I caution him, "But that guy down at the end of the bar, with the short brown hair and the sexy stubble? That's Luke."

"Who?"

"Professor Sexy Pants," I hiss.

"What?! Oh my god, where?!" Danny crows, whipping around in his seat.

"Danny! I told you not to look!" I breathe, grabbing hold of my friend's arm.

"Goddamn, Sophie. You weren't kidding," Danny whistles, "That is one fine specimen of a man, right there."

Despite my better judgment, I peer around Danny to get a second look. Luke is standing along the far side of the bar, leaning up against the rough wooden surface. But even though I'd recognize that sharp jaw and those dark green eyes anywhere, I almost can't believe that this is the same man who's been lecturing me about the economy for the past couple of months.

Gone are the professional slacks and button downs I've grown accustomed to seeing him in. Gone are the nice shoes, the laptop, the stacks of graded papers. Tonight, Luke's barely recognizable in a dark gray tee shirt and dark wash jeans, cut perfectly to his chiseled chest and sculpted ass. His chestnut brown hair is just the right kind of tousled, and even the stubble on his jaw seems darker than it was yesterday. But it isn't just his clothes that have changed since our run-in after class. His entire demeanor is different. He's dropped the upright school hero act entirely. His stance is easy and confident, his body relaxed and supple. Every one of his perfect muscles seems rested and ready for action…of *any* variety. This assured everyman is even more appealing to me than the high and mighty golden boy I've always known Luke to be. Just when I thought he couldn't get any more intriguing…

"Are you gonna go talk to him?" Danny asks excitedly.

"No way. Absolutely not," I say, trying to sound firmer in my convictions that I feel.

"And why the hell not?" Danny presses, "Are you still mad about that little after school chat? He probably just wanted you to stick around so he could check out your tits in that black spandex."

"The chat was one thing," I say, "But that little note he followed up with? That was too much."

"What note was that?" Danny asks, cocking his head.

"The email," I clarify, "I sent it to you."

"No you didn't," Danny replies.

"Sure I did. Right after I read it. Luke sent over some little ditty about how I should consider other career paths so I don't squander my potential," I say, rolling my eyes.

"This is news to me," Danny says, "Are you sure you sent it to the right address?"

"Of course," I tell him, "It's not my fault you only check your email once a week, you Luddite."

"I'm an artist," Danny shrugs, "I'm allowed to be a Luddite. But *you* are not allowed to leave here without talking to Professor Sexy Pants."

"I already told you, I'm not interested," I say, lying through my teeth.

"But fate has brought you together!" Danny whines, wrapping his arms around my waist, "On what other occasion would we find ourselves in a shit hole like this?" He pauses to mouth "I'm sorry" to the scowling bartender before going on, "It's totally meant to be, my dear."

"I assure you, Luke wouldn't agree," I tell my friend, prying his arms from around me, "Now for the love of god, would you please drop it?"

Danny's eyes gleam with mischief as he turns away from me in a huff. Relieved, I lift my glass and take a big swig of my gin and tonic. But before I can swallow properly, Danny's cupped his hands around his mouth and screamed across the bar—

"Hey-a, Luke!"

I promptly choke on my mouthful of gin as Danny hops off his stool, clearing Luke's sightline and scampering off into the crowd. I feel Luke's eyes before I see them, raking hotly along my bare skin. Struggling to compose myself, I lift my gaze and look warily across the bar...but there's no one looking back. Luke's disappeared from his spot. Is he avoiding me completely now? I guess I can't blame him for not wanted to see a student at the bar, but—

"You really shouldn't drink alone, you know," a rich voice says from over my shoulder.

I whip around to see Luke Hawthorne settling down onto the barstool beside mine. Is that excitement I feel at seeing him, or trepidation?

"You're full of advice, aren't you?" I say to him, playing it cool. Who says there aren't practical applications for an acting degree? I knock back the rest of my drink in one big gulp.

"Let me buy you another," Luke says, signaling for the bartender. He's not asking, he's telling.

"Isn't there some kind of rule against fraternizing with students?" I ask him.

"You're not technically my student, according to Sheridan. I was just filling in for an old mentor. And besides, as of this afternoon, my class is over," he reminds me.

"Lucky me," I reply, averting my eyes from Luke's intense gaze.

"Lucky is right," he grins, as the bartender sets two new drinks down in front of us.

I take a healthy sip from my replenished glass, baffled by this new version of Luke Hawthorne. This effortlessly cool bad boy thing of his is totally working for me, and so is the way he's looking at me right now. But I can't let him know that. Not just yet. We've still got a few things to sort out before I let my guard down, here.

"So what's with the getup?" I ask him, raising an eyebrow.

"The getup?" he asks, amused.

"Yeah. I thought your style was Grad school Ken," I shoot back.

"Oh, you were a fan of the collared shirts?" he grins back at me, taking a sip of his bourbon.

"Not exactly," I reply, "This is just...not a side of you I've seen before."

"Well, when have you seen me outside of the classroom?" he asks.

"Just on every Sheridan brochure I've ever flipped through," I tease him.

He groans at the jab, shaking his head.

"Touche," he says, "I should have known that my reputation would precede me."

"And then some," I reply, sipping my drink.

"Oh yeah?" he says, resting his forearms on the bar, just inches from my own. I feel the air between us spark with tension. "What else have you heard about me?"

"I've heard...that you're some kind of iron man when it comes to sports," I reply, ticking off his attributes on my fingers, "I've heard that you're super smart at whatever number crunching it is you're so fond of. And...I've heard that you've got a new lady friend hanging on your arm every other week."

His green eyes gleam rakishly in the dim light of the bar. "Well, I guess I can't exactly refute any of that..." he grins. "But there's a bit more to me than you'll see on the front of a brochure."

"Oh, I don't doubt it," I reply, my voice dipping low in my register as Luke shifts his body closer to mine.

"I have to say, I don't mind seeing your after-school side either," he goes on, giving me a long, intent once-over. I can feel trails of heat skirt across my skin as his eyes travel along my body.

"Oh yeah?" I breathe. It's all I can think to say.

"Yeah," he smiles, letting his arm brush against mine on the bar. "But I'm curious... How is it you ended up at The Bear Trap tonight, Sophia?"

"You can call me Sophie," I say, edging closer toward him. "And I'm here because I couldn't stomach one more college party this year, to be honest."

"Is that so?" Luke asks, his grin widening.

"It is," I reply, swinging my body around so that our knees touch beneath the bar. With every tiny graze, electricity sears through my nerves, ricocheting around my body like a lightning strike.

"Funny that you'd pick a place like this," Luke goes on, glancing around the bar, "It doesn't exactly seem like your scene."

"Until tonight, I'd say the same to you," I point out. "What, does this place have a 'no drama majors' policy or something?"

"I'm just wondering if you didn't have an ulterior motive, showing up at my favorite bar," Luke says, fixing me with his intense gaze.

I don't know if it's the gin, or the noise, or the closeness of Luke's face to mine that has my head spinning. But I *do* know that he's lost me, here.

"First off, I didn't know this was your favorite bar," I tell him, "And secondly, what ulterior motive might I have in mind, Luke?"

"Oh, I don't know if I should say…" he shrugs, taking a swig of his drink, "Come to think of it, I probably need to leave Sheridan and get my ass handed to me in the real world before doling out any more life advice…Am I right? Don't want to sound like a prick, here."

I have to grab hold of the bar to keep from toppling over as Luke's words hit me in the gut. He's quoting my own words back to me, repeating the message I sent Danny earlier this evening, in response to his own email. My breath lodges itself in my throat as I realize my mistake. And Luke lets out a bark of laughter as he watches me realize…

"I think someone hit 'reply' when she meant to hit 'forward'," he laughs, reaching to lay a hand on mine. But I yank my hand away before he can touch me, hiding my trembling fingers in my lap. Luke's brow furrows as I shut him down. "Hey, Sophie…Don't be embarrassed. It's not a big—"

"I have to go," I say quickly, picking myself up from the barstool, "Thanks for the drink, but—"

"Hey, come on…" he says, standing up beside me, "It's not a big deal. I'm actually—"

But I don't stick around to hear what he has to say. I take off across the crowded bar, ducking and weaving around countless boozed-up locals. Humiliation colors my cheeks bright red as I dash away from Luke. How could I have been so stupid? Now he knows exactly how much I've wanted him all semester. He must think I'm a ridiculous little schoolgirl with a crush, for god's sake.

I catch a glimpse of Danny's amber hair by the front door. He's standing very close to a strapping young bloke, already deep in conversation. Knowing full well that I'm being the Queen of Cock Blocks, I rush up to my friend, flustered and panting.

"Danny, we have to go," I breathe, shoving my mess of blonde hair out of my face.

"What happened to you?" Danny asks, cocking an eyebrow.

"Nothing. I. It's just...Can we please get out of here?" I plead, "I just made a huge ass of myself in front of Luke, and—"

"Ooh, this sounds good," says Danny's new friend, turning his attention to me.

"How did you already mess things up with Luke?" Danny demands, "I leave you alone for three minutes, and—"

"That email I meant to send you? About how I want Luke to fuck me dirty? I sent it to *him*," I say in a rush.

Danny and his friend both clap a hand to their mouths, their eyes going wide in unison.

"See? This is why I don't trust technology," Danny says sagely.

"That is *such* an interesting stance..." his friend replies, laying a hand on Danny's bicep.

"Look. I'm calling a cab and getting the hell out of here," I say, glancing over my shoulder to make sure Luke hasn't spotted me. "You can stay, but—"

"No no no," Danny says, shaking his head, "You're not going anywhere."

"What?!" I laugh incredulously, "Says who?"

"Says your best friend," Danny replies, "Your best friend who has been listening to you gush about this guy for months. So what if he knows you're into him? Now all of your cards are on the table."

"But Danny—"

"No 'but Danny's," my friend cuts me off, "You think this guy is sexy as hell, right? So, go back there and see what happens with him already! Would he have come over to talk you up if he wasn't interested too?"

"I...I don't—" I stammer.

"I do," Danny says resolutely, laying his hands on my shoulders, "You were the one who wanted something exciting out of tonight, right? Well, what could be more exciting than hooking up with a guy you're actually into, instead of just going with whatever lame undergrad happens along?"

He has a point. I've never been one to back down when I want something. And good *god* how I've wanted Luke Hawthorne since the second he arrived on the scene. A slow smile spreads across my face as I resolve to give this a try. What's the worst that could happen? It's not like we're going to be seeing each other once the year is out.

"There's the game face I want to see," Danny says, spinning me around and giving me a little shove, "Now *march*."

I take a deep breath and do just that, picking my way back through the crowd with renewed purpose. Thank god for the liquid courage coursing through my blood—I'm gonna need it. Through a sea of burly guys and busty girls, I see that Luke hasn't budged from his spot at the bar... But *my* spot has been filled by an enterprising redhead who's trying to catch his eye. She perches on my vacated stool, fluttering her eyelashes in Luke's direction. Looks like I've swung back around just in the nick of time.

"Luke," I call over the music as I approach.

He turns to see me marching in his direction, pleasantly surprised that I've come around. He swings that perfectly balanced body around on his barstool, eyes gleaming as I zero in on him.

"I was afraid you'd run off," he says, standing to meet me.

"Well, never fear," I grin, stepping up to his tall, broad-shouldered form.

"Did you forget something?" he asks, taking a step toward me. Not an inch of space separates our bodies now. I need to remind myself to keep drawing breath as the hugeness of his presence threatens to overwhelm me.

"Yeah," I breathe, reaching up to take his face in my hands, "I did."

With that, I lift my mouth to his, laying a kiss on those full, firm lips. And wouldn't you know it? He's is kissing me back...and then some. He circles my slender waist with his arms, tugging my body to his in the middle of the crowded bar. No one but the put-out redhead seems to notice as we lock lips. But then again, I'd be hard pressed to notice if the bar was burning down around me with the taste of Luke Hawthorne dancing across my tongue.

I rake my fingers through his short, dark hair, pulling myself flush against him. The panes of his chest are hard against my breasts, which threaten to burst out of my crop top with each heaving breath I take. We need to take cover before we start ripping each other's clothes off. Somehow, I imagine that the other customers might just take notice of that...

"You're not just trying to snag some extra credit are you?" Luke growls, running his hands over the firm rise of my ass.

"Would you object if I was?" I smile back.

"Fuck no," he laughs.

"Well, I can do without the GPA boost," I grin back, "But I'm not done with you just yet, Professor Hawthorne."

"Come on then," he murmurs, taking my hand in his, "This feels more like a one-on-one meeting to me..."

His fingers tighten around mine as he parts the crowd surrounding us, leading me away from the jam packed bar to somewhere a little more private.

Look at that, I think to myself, my body buzzing with anticipation, *Looks like I can let someone else lead after all.*

Chapter Three

I suck in a huge breath as Luke snaps open the clasp of my bra with a flick of his wrist. He runs his hands along my eager body, cupping my breasts with a firm, expert touch. I let my fingertips brush along the muscular v of his waist, eyes fixed on that incredible length straining against his boxer briefs. Bracing myself against the wooden door, I run my hands along his massive cock, groaning as I feel how hard he is.

"Fuck, that's good..." he murmurs, grabbing hold of my hips.

"Yeah?" I smile breathlessly, tracing the outline of his swollen head with my thumb.

"Yeah," he grins, "Here. Let me show you..."

I swallow a cry as he slips a hand up under my red skirt, his knowledgeable fingers brushing against my inner thigh. He lets out a low groan as he traces along the length of my slit, barely covered by my favorite black panties.

"You're already wet for me..." he breathes, kissing down along my neck.

"Can you blame me?" I laugh, working my hands up and down his cock.

"Not even a little," he smiles, kissing me hard on the mouth as he strokes my aching sex.

Our lips move together as we work each other up. Two flimsy layers of cotton are all that separate us from taking the other into our eager hands. I can feel my knees begin to tremble as Luke touches me. I don't know how much longer I can wait to have him, feel him the way I've wanted. The way I've dreamed of. I tug down his dark jeans, steadying myself against the door.

"Well?" I gasp, chest heaving, "I know I said I wanted you to nail me to the wall...but I think a door will do the trick."

"Yeah, I think I can work with that," he grins ravenously, pushing me hard against the flimsy bathroom door.

My heart skips a beat as I feel this controlled hint of his true strength. With that body, those perfectly formed muscles, he could probably curl me with one hand behind his back. I've always wanted to be with a guy who was strong enough to take me on. Someone who's not afraid to be a little physical. A little rough. That's a side of my desire I've never been able to explore with anyone. Until...

A sharp hammering knock on the door makes me jump. Someone's been pounding away out there, refusing to be ignored. Sounds like somebody must really need to break the seal. I've been so wrapped up with Luke that I almost didn't notice before. But now they're yelling above the music...Yelling for *me*.

"Sophie!" someone calls desperately, "Sophie, get out here!"

"Expecting visitors?" Luke asks, brow furrowing slightly.

"Sophie please," the voice entreats me, "I think Danny's in trouble."

It's only then that I recognize the voice as the guy my friend was chatting up not a moment ago. He sounds absolutely terrified.

"Shit," I mutter, hurrying to clasp my bra and straighten my clothes.

"What's going on?" Luke asks as I break away from him.

"My friend needs me," I reply. "I'm sorry, I have to—"

Luke nods silently, struggling to do up his jeans despite his enormous erection. We put aside our case of collective blue balls as I wrench open the bathroom door, coming face-to-face with Danny's new friend. The poor guy has gone completely white, his eyes as wide as dinner plates.

"Where is he?" I demand.

The frightened man points toward the main room of the bar. I turn to see a group of guys forming, closing in around something. Or rather, some*one*.

"Danny," I whisper, taking off at a run.

I tear through the crowd, shoving and shouldering people out of the way as I rush to my friend's side. I come up against a wall of solid muscle as I try to reach him—a perimeter of burly dudes holds me at bay. Through the forest of their beefy torsos, I see Danny standing at the center of it all, blond head held high as some asshole sneers at him, jabbing a finger into his chest.

"We don't take kindly to your type around here," the man snarls, his shaved head glinting dangerously in the low light.

"And what type is that?" Danny challenges him, his fists clenched.

"You know full well," his aggressor goes on, backing Danny across the circle, "I seen you talking up that other little guy. Battin' your eyelashes. I know what you are."

The men around the circle shove Danny forward as he reaches the edge of the circle. I see his jaw pulse with fury as he straightens himself up, unwilling to back down.

"Well, you know what they say," Danny shoots back, leveling his clear-eyed gaze at the pathetic man before him, "It takes one to know one."

Time slows to a crawl as I watch the man's eyes blaze with ire. His hands tighten into punishing fists, and I watch in horror as he cocks back a thick arm.

"*No*," I shout, bursting through the wall of men trying to box me out.

I throw myself into the circle, my shoulder colliding hard with Danny's attacker. I catch him in the ribs, knocking him off balance. He rights himself as I plant my feet firmly on the sawdust-covered ground, standing between Danny and this idiot that would do him harm.

"Look at that!" the man crows, "He's got himself a little guard-bitch!"

A raucous laugh goes up around the circle at my expense, but I couldn't care less.

"You think ten on one is a fair fight?" I snap at him, "Needed all your buddies here to take on my friend? Why don't you just deal with me instead, you prick?"

"Step aside before you get hurt, little girl," the bald man growls back at me, taking a menacing step forward.

"Sophie, get back," Danny urges, grabbing hold of my arm.

"He won't hurt me," I say, my voice raised so the whole bar can hear, "Will you, buddy?"

"My beef ain't with you," he snarls, coming to a stop before me, "It's with your queer little friend, here."

"Is that why you needed all this backup?" Danny laughs, looking at the men looming around us, "You're too afraid to deal with the Big Bad Queer yourself? You homophobic little chicken shit—"

With a roar of outrage, the burly skinhead charges at Danny, ready to draw blood. Adrenaline highjacks my body, and before I know what's happening, I'm letting out a shrill scream and driving the heel of my hand up against the man's nose. A sickening crunch sounds out as my hand makes contact, and the furious man goes reeling away. Blood streams down his face as he clutches his broken nose, staring at me incredulously. I stare back, amazed at what I've done. Guess those self-defense classes at Sheridan really paid off.

"Oh, shit…" Danny whispers, staring at his attacker.

Without flinching, the man grabs hold of his busted nose and works it back into place with a gut-wrenching pop, his eyes blazing with malice. A wild, deranged smile spreads across his bloody face. Something tells me he wouldn't object to hitting a woman now. He lowers his center of gravity, every muscle coiled with irate energy. I brace myself for impact as he bellows out a bloodthirsty wail, lunging toward us across the circle of men.

The skinhead's head snaps back as a thickly muscled arm clotheslines him across the throat. I swing my gaze around to see Lukas Hawthorne's broad back, rippling beneath his charcoal tee shirt. Among all the people looking on, he's the only one who's stepped forward to help Danny and me. His shoulders are raised as he settles into a fighter's stance, waiting for his opponent to pull himself up from the floor. The disgusting man manages to come to standing, eyes going wide as he takes in the sight of Luke standing before him.

"You wanna fight someone?" Luke growls, towering over the bald man, "Well, here I am."

"This has nothing to do with you, Hawthorne," the bloodied man snarls. "It's these two I've got a problem with—Nancy boy and his lipstick-wearing pit bull."

The circle of men edges back as Luke grabs the bald man by the front of his shirt and hoists him off the ground. I gasp as Luke throws his opponent back to the floor, standing over him with pure contempt blazing in his dark green eyes.

"You know I could beat the shit out of you, right Thompson?" Luke barks.

"All right, all right," the man at his feet moans, "You've made your point."

"It's not all right, you fucker," Luke spits, rolling the man onto his back with one steel-toed boot. "How's it feel, getting the shit kicked out of you when you know you don't stand a chance?"

"Lay off already," the man goes on, blathering pathetically.

"Not 'til you apologize to my friends," Luke tells him, laying his heavy boot on the man's chest.

"They're the ones who should apologize!" the skinhead roars, shooting daggers at me and Danny, "Coming in here with their hipster-ass skinny jeans and their big ideas, shoving their pervert ways down our throats. They need to *go*."

"No, Thompson," Luke growls, his voice low and deadly, "You're the one who needs to go."

"Fuck you, Hawthorne," the man spits, "What are you, one of them now?"

"I'd rather be one of them than one of you any day," Luke replies, shoving the man away with his foot. "Now, are you gonna walk out of here on your own?"

"I don't think I will," the bald man says, puffing out his chest as he pulls himself to standing.

"Suit yourself," Luke shrugs.

I jump back as he lunges across the circle and grabs our aggressor by the scruff of his neck. Instead of rushing to the skinhead's defense, the men around us clear a path the door, cheering Luke on. I guess they don't really care who's getting beat up, as long as there's a fight to watch. Someone wrenches open the front door, letting in a burst of warm night air. Without a word, Luke drop kicks Thompson over the threshold. A round of applause and raucous hollering goes up around Luke as he slams the door behind that asshole, brushing off his firm, capable hands.

"Well shit," Danny murmurs behind me, and Luke makes his way toward us, "Looks like you caught yourself a keeper, Sophie Porter."

"Luke…" I breathe, as he stops before us, "I…I don't know what to say."

"I do," Danny cuts in, "Thank you, man."

"Of course," Luke shrugs, "Just keeping the trash out as best I can. I like this place too much to see it overrun with idiots."

"I'm so sorry this happened Danny," I tell my friend, lacing my fingers through his.

"It's OK. I'm all right," he assures me, "I'd just…I'd like to get out of here now."

"Of course," I reply, squeezing his hand, "Let's call a cab."

"I could drive you," Luke offers, nodding toward the door, "My car's out front."

"No, it's OK," I tell him, not wanting to impose. "I think you've done enough for us tonight."

His brow furrows as he looks at me, the expression on his sculpted face totally unreadable.

"Whatever you say," he says evenly, tucking his hands into the pockets of his jeans.

Between our mind-scrambling make out session and the jarring conflict with that asshole, I'm feeling totally disoriented. Part of me wants desperately to stay here and see what happens with Luke, but the rest of me is way too unsettled by what just happened to see this night through. I'm sure that if Luke wants to see me again after tonight, he'll let me know. But for right now, I just need to get out of here and get Danny to safety. I owe him that.

"Cab's on its way," Danny murmurs, after pressing a few keys on his smart phone. "I should find Greg and say goodbye."

He holds out his hand to Luke, who gives it a firm shake. Without another word, Danny moves off into the crowd in search of his friend. I cross my arms tightly across my chest, my eyes glued to the floor as I stand awkwardly beside Luke. Just a couple of hours ago, he was just my handsome, arrogant teacher, all ironed shirts and unwarranted advice. I knew how to handle myself around him. But the Luke I met tonight—the man who knew how to turn me on with a single touch, who was ready to jump to a total stranger's defense because it was the right thing to do—he's unlike anyone I've ever met. And suddenly, I feel like I've forgotten all my lines in the middle of a scene.

"You're quiet all of a sudden," Luke observes, laying a hand on my arm.

"Just a little rattled I guess," I manage, keeping my eyes averted.

He withdraws his hand, staring at me with that same indiscernible look.

"That's fair," he nods, looking away from me.

I bite my lip, feeling as though I've said something wrong. He doesn't think I'm upset about what happened between *us*, does he?

"Luke, I—" I begin, but a waving arm catches my eye across the room. Danny's flagging me down to let me know the cab is here.

"You'd better get a move on," Luke says to me, running a hand through his short dark hair. "Get home safe, OK?"

"Um. Yeah," I stammer helplessly. "But…Luke?"

"Hmm?"

"We're cool, right? I mean—"

"Of course we are," he says with a placid half smile, "Have a good summer, Sophie."

And just like that, turns and walks away. I stare after him, totally at a loss. What the hell just happened here?

"Sophie, come on!" Danny calls from across the crowded bar.

I turn on my heel and hurry for the door, eyes prickling with sudden, surprising tears. Am I angry at having my time with Luke interrupted by some ignorant asshole? Or am I disappointed that he didn't ask to see me again? Or am I still just hopelessly turned on and in need of a major self-love session once I get home?

Whatever has me upset, I know I'll be able to deal with it much better once we've made it out of The Bear Trap. Clasping hands, Danny and I hurry out the front door and into the waiting cab. We ride along toward the relative safety of campus in silence.

"I don't know about you," Danny finally says, "But that's enough excitement for me tonight."

"Yeah," I murmur, still attempting to blink back my tears, "A shitty Disney movie doesn't seem too bad right about now."

"I have *Hercules* on DVD and a bottle of Merlot at my place," Danny offers.

"Done," I smile back at him, glad for a spot of levity. We could use it after the intense, startling night we both had.

"So...how did you leave things with the Professor?" Danny asks after a moment.

"I'm not even sure," I tell him, "But I'm pretty sure I managed to fuck it up."

"Wow. In just one night? That's a new record for you," Danny laughs weakly.

"You know me," I sigh, sinking against the backseat as we race along the highway, "Always gotta outdo myself somehow."

***

The campus is nearly deserted the next morning when I finally make my way home from Danny's place. We fell asleep watching cartoons and drinking cheap wine like we were wee little freshmen again—but then, we both needed a little bit of comfort after the events of last night. Already, everything that happened at The Bear Trap feels like a dream—a sexy, scary, unsettling dream. For the first time, I find myself wondering whether I *am* ready to deal with the world outside my cozy university walls. After all, there may not always be a Luke Hawthorne to rush to my rescue.

Luke weighs heavily on my mind as I arrive back at my dorm to find that my roommate Kim has already moved her things out of our shared abode. Though we barely traded more than a few niceties over the course of the year, I find myself feeling unaccountably lonely here in my half-empty dorm room. But then, maybe it's not just anybody's company I'm longing for now. Maybe it's the company of a certain sexy professor—the man who saved me and my best friend from god knows what last night. The memory of Luke's hands, the way his body felt against mine, comes roaring back to me, and I hurry to sit down at my desk before I topple over with longing.

I eagerly open my laptop to see if he's reached out to me since last night. But when I scan my email inbox, there's no new message from Luke Hawthorne. My heart sinks as I sit back in my chair, unreasonably disappointed. My fear that I bungled things between us last night burrows deeper into my heart. It's not like we promised to keep in touch or anything, now that school is over. What was I expecting? What do I even want from him, come to think of it?

As I stare despondently at my computer screen, a new message appears in my inbox. My heart leaps into my throat as I hurry to open it, sure that it's Luke checking up on me…But no dice. The email is from my mother, Robin Porter. I open it up and read a short message, written in her typical scatterbrained syntax.

```
Hi Sophie girl! Happy summer!! Can't
wait to see you for family vaca. Did I
remember to give you the address? The
lake house is gorg, you're going to
```

love it. Hmm… Actually need to LOOK UP
the address first, but I'll get it to
you eventually. See you in a week baby
love you!!1 Mom

I let my head fall into my hands as my mother's email
jogs my memory. Of course. The family vacation. With all
the hustle around the end of the semester, I nearly forgot
that my mom has planned some big reunion for me and my
two sisters in a week's time.

Our mom has been here in Montana for nearly a
month already, spending some time in her hometown of
old to "ground herself" or something. Really, I think she
just needed to get out of Vermont, and away from the
house she used to share with Dad. His death three years
ago totally leveled her, caused her to become even more
flighty and erratic than she had been while we were
growing up.

Mom's a visual artist, and a pretty decent one too.
She was always the fun, unpredictable parent while my
father, Archie, was the source of our stability. They really
did balance each other well. Neither was perfect, but they
were perfect for each other. When we lost Dad, Mom lost
that sense of balance entirely. By the time I headed off to
school, she was already sleeping around again, inviting
men back to the house on a whim, taking off on
unannounced "trips" despite the fact that my little sister
Annabel was only sixteen.

This inconsiderate streak of my mother's is
something I've learned to work around out of necessity.
Since Dad died, I've gone out of my way to spend as much
time here at school as possible. I even stopped going home
for the summers, claiming that I wanted to take extra
classes in order to graduate early. And while there may be
a nugget of truth in that, the real reason I don't go back to
Vermont anymore is because it's just too painful. I need to
keep distance between me and my family, for the sake of

my own mental health. My older sister Maddie is doing the same thing by settling down in Seattle, whether she realizes it or not. Grief may unite some families, but it's flung us Porter women all across the country.

Of course, I couldn't very well say no to a family vacation when my mom planned for it to take place just a couple hours away. I begrudgingly agreed to her little adventure, then immediately put it out of mind. No getting out of it now, though. It looks like I'm headed into the backwoods for two weeks of awkward family bonding.

Between the impending reunion and the fiasco that was last night, this summer's really getting off to a good start, huh?

Chapter Four

Outside of Kalispell, MT

One Week Later…

Squinting in the bright afternoon sun, I trudge along the narrow shoulder of the highway with my heavy backpack weighing me down. I don't own a car, so my only way of getting to this middle-of-nowhere lake house my mother rented was to take a bus from Sheridan. Little did I know that the "nearby bus stop" my mom swore existed would be three miles away from my final destination.

So far, this vacation is definitely living up to my expectations.

My caramel hair is plastered to my sunburnt forehead, my shoulders aching with lugging my pack along. If I knew I'd be hiking to our vacation spot, I would have left *War and Peace* behind in my dorm room. Nothing to be done now, I guess. If my mom's directions are right (which at this point is anyone's guess) the house should be just a ways down the dirt road coming up on my right. I pause to rest before the final leg of my long walk, letting my backpack fall to the hot pavement with a thud. Just as I unburden myself, I spot a pickup truck rumbling down the road toward me.

And it looks to be slowing down.

"Great," I mutter as the truck approaches.

I've gotten more than enough catcalls, whistles, and offers to trade a ride for a blowjob today. Montana boys can be just as forward as any big city man, that's for damn sure. I cross my arms, trying to signal the driver that I'm not interested in being harassed today. But, big surprise, he doesn't pick up on the hint.

"Hey there," says a man's voice over the pickup's engine, "Are you—?"

"No," I cut off the driver, "I'm not lost, I don't need a ride, and I don't have any cash, grass, or ass to spare. So you can keep on trucking, pal."

The man behind the wheel lifts the brim of his baseball cap, revealing a stoic but handsome face halfway obscured by a bushy, salt and pepper beard.

"Actually, I was going to ask if you were Sophie Porter," the man replies.

I look up at him sharply, taken aback. "How do you—?"

"Thought so," he nods, "You look just like Robin when she was your age."

"I'm sorry...*Who* are you?" I ask. I wouldn't know this man from Adam—how is it that he knows both my and my mother's name?

"Apologies," he goes on, "Shoulda introduced myself. Name's John. I'm an old school friend of your mother's."

"Oh," I reply, "That's...nice."

"Sure is," John chuckles, "She told me you were coming in on the bus, so I came out to meet you. That woman may be a good painter, but she can't read a map for shit."

"That's for sure," I smile tentatively.

"Sorry you still had to walk most of the way," John goes on, "Come on. Let me give you a lift back to the house."

"Um. All right," I agree, approaching the truck and wrenching open the rusty door. "You know where this lake house is, then?"

"I sure hope so," John laughs gruffly as I climb up into the truck, "I built the damn thing."

"You built...the house we're renting?" I ask him, totally lost.

"Ah," he grumbles, pulling off onto the dirt road, "Guess Robin left out a couple details about this little trip."

"Guess so," I reply, sinking back against the passenger's seat, "Care to fill me in?"

"Well," John starts, "The long and the short of it is, your Mom's been staying with me while she's back in town. She called up a couple months back and let me know she was coming home for a spell. I told her she could crash with me while she spent some time getting back to her roots."

"Mom's been living with you this whole time?" I ask him, eyes wide.

"Yep," the man replies, "Like I told you, we go way back, Robin and me. Grew up in this little town together. Used to be thick as thieves, once upon a time."

"Uh-huh," I say flatly.

Something tells me that John and my mom are thicker than ever, if she's been living out here in the woods with

him—for months. Without letting any of her daughters know. I've managed to avoid meeting too many of Mom's little boyfriends since Dad passed away, but it looks like my lucky streak has just come to an end.

"I didn't realize this would all be news to you," John says, stealing a glance at me, "I hope you can still enjoy yourself here. How long are you staying?"

"Two weeks," I tell him. *And not a second longer,* I add silently to myself.

"Plenty of time to kick back and relax," he smiles, "I really think you'll like it here. The house is plenty big for the whole lot of us. My boys aren't exactly the most socialized creatures you'll ever meet, but they're harmless. Mostly they just keep to themselves."

"Your...boys?" I ask.

"My sons," John nods, "Got three of 'em. Otherwise known as 'a handful'."

"I'm sure," I reply, trying not to sound annoyed. It's bad enough that I'm stuck here in the boonies for two weeks. Now I have to deal with some rowdy trio of country guys smashing beer cans against their foreheads, and stalking around with BB guns, or...whatever it is men do when left to their own devices?

Just as the silence between John and I reaches the point of being comfortably long, he turns off onto a long driveway lined with trees.

"Here we are," he says proudly, "Home sweet home."

I peer through the windshield, expecting some rickety lean-to or dilapidated farm house. But what I lay eyes on instead takes my breath away.

John's house is a gorgeous, three story masterpiece. It strikes the perfect balance between rustic and elegant, and through the trees beyond it I can see a sprawling, crystal blue lake. The house's well-made wooden exterior is a rich, deep brown, spotted with dark green shutters that—I can't help but notice—are the same color as Luke Hawthorne's eyes.

Get a grip, Sophie, I chide myself, *You're supposed to be getting over Luke while you're here, not dwelling on him every waking moment.*

But getting over Luke Hawthorne has proven to be easier said than done this past week. I haven't heard a word from him since our steamy run-in at The Bear Trap. God, if only our little tryst hadn't been cut short by that awful asshole who was harassing Danny. If Luke and I had been alone for five more minutes...

No. It doesn't bear thinking about. If he wanted to see me again, he would have gotten in touch with me by now. He has my email address, doesn't he? Granted, I also have his, but I can't very well be the first one to reach out. Not after I acted like such a weirdo at the end of the night. It's time to face the facts: I totally botched my one shot at getting it on with Luke Hawthorne, and now I have to get over it, whether I like it or not.

"John, this place is gorgeous," I finally manage to say once I've forced Luke Hawthorne from my mind once more.

"Thank you," the man replies, bringing the pickup truck to a stop and swinging down from the driver's seat. When I scramble down after him, I see that he's built like a grizzly bear, tall and imposing. I can't help but be a little intimidated by him, to be honest. But after the other night at the bar, I can say that I've met scarier guys than him. Thank god I had someone to stand up for me when I did.

I follow John around the house, admiring the wide covered verandah that circles the house. He leads me up the stairs to the back patio, and I pause to take in the gorgeous view of the lake. The smooth water reflects the horizon back on itself, each tree, hill, and cloud cast in striking double relief. For the first time, I manage to give this trip the benefit of the doubt. Maybe spending some time in such a beautiful place, removed from the stresses of school, friends, and my baffling love life will do me some good after all.

"Is that Sophie?!" I hear my mother's voice trill from inside the house.

Before I can even turn around, I'm being smothered by a cloud of golden blonde curls and airy, girlish laughter.

"Hello to you too, Mom," I reply, pulling away from her ardent embrace to get a look at her.

No matter how much time goes by between our visits, my mother never seems to age. John was right when he said that we look alike. With her slender figure, smooth skin, and playful blue eyes run through with hints of gold, she looks more like my sister than my mother. And more often than not, she acts like it, too.

"I'm so happy to see you, baby!" Mom beams, clapping a hand to her flushed cheek. "It's been...God, how long *has* it been?"

"Just since Christmas, Mom," I reply, adjusting my backpack on my tired shoulders.

"Here, let me take that," John says, lifting the bag from my back, "I'll put it upstairs in one of the spare bedrooms."

"Oh. Sure," I tell him, receiving a gruff nod in reply.

"Thanks for going to pick her up," my mom says to John, laying a tender hand on his bulging bicep, "You're the best."

"Yeah, yeah," John grumbles amiably, "So you keep telling me."

I wait until our brawny host has disappeared into the lake house before rounding on my mother.

"Funny thing," I say wryly, "I don't remember you mentioning your pet lumberjack, when you invited me out here."

"Pet lumberjack?" my mom echoes, cocking her head at me, "You mean John?"

"Yes, of course I mean John," I reply, "A little warning would have been nice, Mom."

"I could have sworn I told you..." she says absently, looking out across the wide lawn.

"No," I tell her, "You didn't."

"Well...Surprise!" she laughs, clasping her hands together, "Isn't he just the sweetest man you've ever met in your life?"

Nope. That would have been Dad, I think to myself, resisting the temptation to say so out loud.

"John's been so kind to me since I've been back in town," my mom goes on, "Really, I don't know what I would have done without him."

"Yeah. He mentioned you guys were old friends," I reply.

"Is *that* what he told you?" Mom asks, eyebrows raised.

"Why," I ask, "Is there more to the story?"

"Oh look!" Mom gushes, ignoring my question completely, "Here comes your sister!"

I spin around on the patio and catch a flash of platinum blonde in the sunlight. Walking up the long dock that stretches into the lake is my little sister, Annabel. Though "little" is hardly the right world for her anymore. At nineteen, she's already the tallest of all the Porter women, with long willowy limbs and big, beautiful doe eyes. All three of us girls were toe heads when we were little, but only Anna retained her bright blonde locks as she grew older. I haven't seen her since the holidays, and in the past several months she's come to look more like a grown woman than ever.

"Look, Anna! Sophie's here!" my Mom trills as Annabel makes her way toward us across the grassy lawn.

"Yeah. I see that, Mom," Anna replies, climbing the patio steps, "What's up, Soph?"

"Not too much. Just got in," I tell her, a little put off by her nonchalance.

Anna's never been super affectionate, even when she was a kid. I respect her utter lack of bullshit, but sometimes I can't help but wish for a big, giddy reunion with my little sister. I really do miss her when I'm away at school. With only two years separating us in age, Anna and I were best friends until we both hit our angsty teenage years. I always hoped that we'd reconnect once we were a little older, but Dad's death and my moving away scattered any chance of that. I often feel like my little sister resents me for leaving her alone with Mom these past three years. And to be perfectly honest, I wouldn't blame her if she did.

"Why don't you show your sister around the place?" Mom says to Anna, all but skipping away into the house.

"Sure," Anna replies, watching her go, "No problem."

The back door slams behind our mother, and Anna and I are alone at last. I jerk my head toward the house, wiggling my eyebrows conspiratorially.

"So, what's the deal with that?" I ask her.

"What, Mom and John?" she replies, "You're asking the wrong person. I didn't even know she was staying with him until I got in from Vermont."

"You mean she didn't even tell *you*?" I ask, gaping at my little sister, "But…you guys still live in the same house!"

"Eh. Nominally," Anna shrugs, "I stopped trying to keep track of her years ago. It's better to just let her do her own thing. You know she's going to anyway."

"Christ. You sound more like the mother than she does," I murmur, crossing my arms.

"Well," Anna replies, "Someone has to be the mom in our relationship, right?"

Sympathy wrings my heartstrings as I reflect for the millionth time on how hard these past few years must have been on Anna. I wish there was some way to talk to her about it, find out how she's really doing. But she's become so closed off to me and Maddie that I wouldn't even know where to begin.

"So, you want to see this place or what?" Anna asks, walking past me toward the house.

"Oh. Uh. Sure," I reply, trailing behind her, "Might as well."

Despite my reservations about this trip, I can't help but be impressed by John's lakeside home. The sprawling interior features a palatial great room with two fireplaces, an incredible, fully stocked kitchen, and more than half a dozen guest rooms. The decor strikes just the right balance between rustic and modern, and it's far more tidy than I would expect, what with four men living here and all. Speaking of all those men…

"Where are these sons I've heard about?" I ask Anna, as we wrap up our tour in the guest bedroom I've been assigned.

"I barely caught a glimpse of them when I got here this morning," she tells me, settling down on the quilt-covered twin bed, "The two younger ones are off camping tonight. They're getting back tomorrow afternoon. And the oldest one hasn't even shown up yet."

"What are they like?" I ask her, sitting cross-legged on the bed. I'll take my sisterly girl talk whenever I can get it.

"Tough to say," she shrugs, "They're pretty quiet. Barely said a word to me before they left. Real hot though."

"Oh yeah?" I press.

"Yeah," she replies, her long platinum hair falling across her face as she glances down at her hands. So much for girl talk. Maybe a different line of questioning would go over better?

"So…How has your gap year been so far?" I ask her. Rather than starting college right away, Anna decided to take a year off. She's a wonderful photographer, and has been building up quite the portfolio in the lead up to applying for art school. If that's what she decides to do, that is.

"You really don't have to do that," she mutters, looking up at me sharply.

"Do what?" I reply, taken aback.

"Make small talk with me," she goes on, "I'm your sister, not your dentist."

"Well, you're not really giving me an opening Anna," I reply, "I'm just trying to—"

"Look," she cuts me off, "Things are going to be weird between us, Sophie. It's inevitable. I just wish you wouldn't try to muscle through it. You're supposed to be the one other Porter woman who's as allergic to bullshit as I am, right?"

"What," I reply, a sly smile spreading across my face, "You don't want me to puke rainbows and butterflies all over you like Mom does?"

"Or obsess about saying the perfect thing—at the perfect time—to the point of insanity, like Maddie," she adds, invoking our older sister's pathological tendency for perfectionism.

I laugh, relishing this taste of my and Anna's childhood dynamic. Madeleine is three years older than me, and claimed Dad as her best friend long before I or Annabel showed up on the scene. With Mom off in the clouds, Anna and I were left to our own devices most of the time, and the friendship that sprung up between us is deeper than any I've ever known. Maybe there's hope for us yet?

"Just be real with me, Sophie," Anna goes on, fixing her big blue eyes on my face, "Isn't that what your fancy drama school is supposed to be teaching you how to do?"

"Sure, onstage," I laugh, "Real life is far more complicated."

"Tell me about it," she sighs, lying back on the twin bed.

I lay down beside her, staring up at the gently spinning ceiling fan. In this moment, I can feel the distance between us collapse just a hair. What I wouldn't give to feel that closeness that used to be such a given between us again.

"For real then," I say to her, turning my face toward hers on the pillow, "How are you actually doing, Annabel?"

"For real?" she replies, rolling onto her side to face me, "Better, lately. Being out of that hell hole of a high school has helped."

"No kidding," I laugh, "That place couldn't handle you, anyway."

"It's more that I was bored stiff by the end," she tells me, "The whole thing just felt so…irrelevant, after Dad…"

"Yeah," I say softly, "I don't know how I would have faked giving a shit about prom and college applications and whatever after losing him."

"You're lucky," she says, "You got to go off and study something you actually cared about. Imagine trying to sit through abstinence-only sex ed while your entire world was being blown apart."

"Good lord," I groan, "They're still doing abstinence only? Are they out of their minds?"

"Just very, very repressed," she says, rolling her eyes, "How did we get stuck in the only conservative bubble in Vermont, I ask you?"

"Just lucky I guess," I smile ruefully. "But you're free now, right?"

"Right. And since Mom's been away playing Backwoods Barbie, I've had the farmhouse to myself, too."

A twinge of jealousy runs through me at this. The Porter family home is built on a sprawling piece of farmland in rural Vermont. Mom and Dad found the place just after he got his first teaching job at a university nearby, and spent the next twenty years building it into their dream home. Mom had plenty of space to paint and sculpt, and the three of us girls had full reign of the fields and woods all around. It really was something of a dream…before.

"I'm really glad you decided to come out here, Soph," Anna goes on, a rare hint of softness coming into her voice.

"Me too," I tell her, "Even taking Mom's little surprise into account. I really needed to get off campus for a second, myself."

"How come?" she asks.

"Oh, just some boring boy trouble..." I tell her vaguely.

"Go on..." she presses, pulling herself onto an elbow.

"Well," I sigh, doing the same, "I *may* have gone and gotten myself a little crush on one of my teaching assistants..."

"Yeah, that sounds like you," she observes.

"And I *may* have made out with him in the bathroom of a bar on the last night of classes," I go on.

"Uh huh. Still follows," she nods.

"And I *may* be having a little trouble thinking about anything but how much I want to jump his bones," I finish in a rush, rolling miserably onto my back.

"Damn," Anna whistles, "I don't think I've ever seen you hung up on a guy like this."

"That's because he's not just any guy," I confide in her, "Seriously, Anna. This dude is perfect. He's smart, and gorgeous, and he stands up for the right thing no matter what. And you should see the size of his—"

"OK, OK, I get the picture. He's perfect," she cuts me off, "But if you're so nuts about him, what's the problem? I've never known you to hold back on going after whatever guy struck your fancy."

"It's different with him," I tell her, "I'm used to guys falling all over themselves for a chance to get in my pants. I've never had to work at snagging one before. But his guy? He's...harder to get a read on, I guess."

"Maybe now you'll know what it feels like to be a mere mortal, where men are concerned," Anna teases me, "Now that your sex goddess jig is up."

"You should talk," I shoot back, "Have you *seen* yourself lately? When the hell did you get drop dead gorgeous?"

"Changing the subject, are we?" she grins, "Fine. But if you need to unburden your aching heart...Make sure to find another sounding board. I can't stand that mushy shit."

"There's the Anna I know and tolerate," I laugh, giving her a shove off the bed.

"At your service," she smiles, springing up on her mile-long legs and heading for the door, "Now, if you'll excuse me, this welcome wagon has reached the end of its line."

She disappears down the hall, leaving me alone at last. The quiet of the woods is almost startling, after living with hundreds of rowdy undergrads all year. In the gathering silence, I find it nearly impossible to drag my thoughts away from Luke Hawthorne once more. Letting Anna in on my secret romance only underlined the extent to which I've been pining for him. She's right. I've never been this hung up on a guy before. Maybe I should just do something about it already, instead of waiting for him to come around. What's the worst that could happen?

Energized, I spring across the room and dig my cellphone out of my backpack. No new messages, but I won't let that deter me this time. I sit down on the bedroom floor and open my email, pulling up a new message window and keying in Luke's address. Here goes nothing.

Hey Luke,

Sophie here. Just wanted to see how you were doing, after everything that happened at The Bear Trap. Sorry for not getting in touch sooner, I guess I was a little embarrassed about how I left things with you. Anyway, I'll be back on campus in a couple of weeks for summer classes. If you'll be in the area and want to hang out, just let me

know. I'd love to pick things up where
we left off.

    Cheers,
    Sophie Porter

"That'll do for now," I mutter, setting the phone on
my bedside table, "The ball's in your court, Professor
Hawthorne."

I set off to explore the property on my own, since
Anna's nowhere to be found. Maybe a nice hike in the
woods will distract me from the longing ache twisting my
core at the very thought of my illusive, almost-lover.

Maybe.

Chapter Five

I don't see much of my housemates for the rest of the night. Anna keeps herself busy, wandering around the expansive property with her camera, and Mom and John sit on the verandah together, drinking and talking in hushed tones. Not that I mind a little me-time after a long day of travel. The peace and quiet will give me some time to settle into my new digs.

Returning to my bedroom just after ten, I decide to indulge in a late-night yoga session to sooth my weary muscles. I go to fetch my travel mat from the depths of my backpack, and absentmindedly glance at my phone en route. There's a message waiting for me. It's probably from Maddie, who's put off joining us until tomorrow, most likely out of self-preservation. Of all us sisters, Maddie clashes with Mom the most violently. I unlock my phone and glance down at the text, but it isn't from my sister at all. It's from a number I've never seen before.

```
Hey. How's it going?
```

Before I can ask who's on the other side of the text, a follow up message appears on my screen.

```
It's Luke, btw. Your cell number's
part of your email signature. Hope it's
cool I texted.
```

My heart flies into my throat as I stare down at those wonderful words. It's only been a week since I've heard from Luke, but my body responds like a long lost love has just come back to me after ten years at sea. With trembling fingers, I tap out a reply.

Me: Hey Luke. Ofc it's cool—I'm glad to hear from you. All well?

Luke: Yeah, can't complain. Enjoying some time off. You?

Me: Same, kind of. Off on a good ol' family vacation. (Kill me.)

Luke: Hahaha, I know that game. Hang in there. It'll be over soon. You'll be back at Sheridan before long, right?

Me: Yep. In a couple of weeks.

Luke: That's good. I'll be working on campus all summer myself. And I miss seeing you.

I grant myself a moment of happy-dancing around my new bedroom. Holy crap—Luke Hawthorne misses me? Composing myself as best I can, I text him back.

Me: Even after my less-than-graceful exit from The Bear Trap the other night?

Luke: Hey, it was a crazy night. I don't blame you for getting freaked out. I just hope our little "private moment" wasn't what spooked you.

Me: Not at all. It was mostly the deranged skinhead. I rather enjoyed getting a private moment with you, tbh.

Luke: That makes two of us, then. I wouldn't mind picking things up where we left off when you get back, either.

There he goes, quoting my own emails back to me again. Not that I mind, given the sentiment.

Me: Is that so?

Luke: Oh, it is. I haven't stopped thinking about the other night. How good it felt to finally get my hands on you.

I have to sit down on my bed as a huge pang of lust shoots through me. That spot between my legs starts pulsing with want, just remembering what it was like to give myself over to Luke. I lay back on the narrow bed and reply...

Me: That's good to know... Because I can't stop thinking about you, either. Especially what you could have done with those hands if we hadn't been interrupted.

Luke: Yeah? You wanted me to keep touching you?

Me: I did. I really did.

Luke: I wanted even more than that, if I'm being honest.

Me: Tell me.

Luke: Sure you can handle it?

Me: I'm sure.

Luke: All right. Honestly, I wanted to push you up against that door and fuck you until you screamed.

A gasp escapes my lips as I read Luke's text. This was not what I was expecting from our little correspondence, but hey—I'll take it.

Me: That would have been so hot…

Luke: Does it get you hot, thinking about me driving my cock up inside of you?

Me: God yes. I might have to take care of myself right now just picturing it.

Luke: Oh man. I love the thought of you touching yourself while you text me…

In that case, I think with a smile, double checking to make sure I locked my bedroom door. Slowly, I let my knees fall open, trailing my fingertips along my taut stomach and under the elastic waist of my cotton shorts. I'm not surprised to find that I'm already wet just thinking about Luke Hawthorne taking me hard and fast from behind. I trace my fingers along the length of my slit, revving myself up as my imagination runs wild. A new text from Luke appears on my phone:

Luke: Are you touching yourself right now?

It takes me a minute in my distracted state, but I manage to respond:

Me: Yes…

Luke: Keep going. Imagine me grabbing you by the hair as I pound into you, pulling just hard enough for you to really feel it.

Me: That's what I want. I want you to be a little rough with me.

Luke: Then think about my fingers digging into your hips as I bear down on you. Imagine my cock splitting you open, hitting you so hard and deep that you almost can't stand it.

My mouth falls open as I bring my fingers up to my throbbing clit. I trace quick, deliciously firm circles over that aching button as I picture Luke poised above me, his perfect body straining with devastating lust.

Luke: Now think of us alone in that lecture hall again. Imagine me flipping you over and laying you out across the desk, totally naked. Think of me bringing my mouth to your pussy, and rolling my tongue over your clit…

I let the phone drop from my hand as warm sensation mounts in the pit of my belly, threatening to spill over. Though my knees begin to quiver, I press on, sending myself hurtling over the edge. A sweeping orgasm rolls through my body. I come hard thinking of Luke's mouth against my sex, and have to bite my lip to keep from moaning so loud the whole house will hear me. Falling back against the bed, I stare up at the ceiling, amazed at what Luke can do to me through texts alone.

My cell chirps beside me, and I pick up in a daze.

```
Luke: That did the trick, huh?

Me: And then some.

Luke: Glad to be of service.

Me: Hold on though...

Luke: What?

Me: You never let me get into what
I'd do to you...

Luke: By all means, share with the
class.
```

I roll onto my stomach, grinning as I let my dirtiest fantasies fly. The hours wear on as Luke and I text well into the night, each of us gunning to get the other off as many times as we can. By the time I finally pass out, my entire body is spent and satisfied. I didn't realize how much tension my body had stored up since the last time I saw Luke. But until I get to see him again in the flesh, I'm more than amenable to this particular form of stress relief.

***

The next morning, I wake up feeling like a brand new woman. I all but spring out of bed, make myself a delicious cup of strong coffee, and take it out to the dock just as the sun is rising. I bask in the light of the breaking day, feeling happier than I have in months. Years? And all because I have something to look forward to again, once I arrive back at school. Nothing can crush my good mood today.

After a nice long shower and lunch with Annabel, I decide to make good on that yoga session I had planned for last night. Not that I mind it being derailed for a steamy sexting session with the hottest man I've ever met, of course. I have to say, I was blown away by the intensity of Luke's plans for me. The way he laid out exactly how he'd work me over. There was a raw, ferocious need in those images he rolled out. I've never been with a guy who wasn't afraid to get a little dirty. These two weeks are going to be the longest of my life.

It's late afternoon by the time I begin my yoga practice on the verandah. In the calm quiet of the woods, I lose myself in my breathing, letting my mind go blissfully blank. The minutes fly by as I move through my favorite sequences of stretches, luxuriating in the poses. So wrapped up am I in my practice, that I don't even notice that someone's approaching until they let out a little shriek of surprise as spotting my twisted limbs on the deck.

"Jesus Christ!" someone yelps from the top of the stairs.

I look up from my pose, a little annoyed at the abrupt interruption. But I guess I should have anticipated it, knowing my older sister was bound to arrive at some point today.

"Oh. Hey, Maddie," I say, swimming up of my blissed-out reverie. "One sec, I'm just finishing up my practice."

"What are you practicing, exactly?" she asks me tersely, watching as I unfold my body, "How to fit a corpse into a suitcase?"

I sit up to face her, failing to swallow a sigh. Madeleine stands staring down at me with a skeptical look—her resting expression, as it were. Though she's a few years older than me, she's as many inches shorter. Often mistaken for the youngest of all us sisters, her body is petite and compact where mine is athletically curvy. I used to get grumpy about her adorably sexy physique, but I've grown to love my womanly body as I've moved out of my teenage years. What I've never grown to love is the patronizing tone my older sister takes with me when she's trying to keep things chipper.

"It's yoga, Maddie," I tell her flatly, "Surely you've heard of it."

The corners of her mouth turn down at my curt response. I can see her fighting the urge to roll her gold-flecked blue eyes—the same eyes that our mother passed down to all three of her daughters. With Herculean restraint, she stops herself from bickering with me right from the get-go. We've always had a way of getting on each other's last nerve from the start.

"Did you know this place was going to be a mansion?" she asks finally, crossing her arms, "There's no way Mom can be affording this easily."

Oh, dear. It looks like Maddie wasn't briefed about the details of this trip either. She has no idea about John, or his sons, or the fact that our mother has been living here for the past couple of months or so. On the bright side, I get to watch her head explode as she learns the true nature of this little getaway. Maddie is an obsessive over-thinker, phased by the smallest wrinkle in her plans. I can't help but be a tiny bit amused as she unknowingly steps up to a wrinkle the size of a mountain.

Sure enough, my older sister's mind promptly melts as our mother sweeps in and divulges the salacious details of her stay in Montana. Anna and I trail along as Maddie is introduced to John—the latest of Mom's unlikely paramours. To her credit, Maddie keeps it together just long enough for us girls to escape into the backyard. When the levees finally break, I'm there to lend her a shoulder to cry on. I forget how hard Dad's death hit her sometimes. He really was her hero, her role model. Seeing Mom with another man is harder on her than it is on me.

Luckily, something comes along to distract all of us Porter girls from our discomfort. Finally, we get to meet one of John's sons in the flesh. He roars up out of the woods on an ATV, nearly mowing us over in the process. Anna wasn't kidding about these boys being hot as hell. This one, who tells us his name is Cash, has the bad boy biker thing down pat. His body is covered in heavy black ink, and his dark curly hair hangs just above his collar. Definitely easy on the eyes, but not really my type. The second he opens his mouth, I can tell there's more brawn than brains to him.

What can I say? I like my men sharp.

Things cool down a bit as the four of us Porter women set to making dinner. John's expecting his two younger sons home tonight, so it'll be the first time that all eight of us will be in the same place at once. My mom is fluttering around the kitchen like a deranged 50's housewife, bent on everything being perfect for our first big group dinner. Maddie's lost in her own thoughts as she hacks away at a pile of vegetables, and Anna is quiet as a mouse as she makes sure Mom doesn't accidentally lose a finger or something in her frenzy.

Me? I make myself comfortable with a glass of Merlot at the rough-hewn kitchen table. Someone's got to taste-test the wine pairings for tonight, right?

"Maddie," our mom chirps as she puts the finishing touches on her feast, "Why don't you go round up the boys? Everything'll be ready in a sec."

My older sister promptly drops her knife, the color draining from her face.

"Oh. I don't. I mean—" she sputters, even more flustered than usual, "I don't really know where they are…"

"I think they're down by the lake," Anna replies, plucking a tray of dinner rolls out of the oven.

I didn't even realize the younger boys had returned from their camping expedition. We haven't gotten so much as a grunt out of any of them, much less a "hello". But after catching a glimpse of the sexy, brooding Cash this afternoon, I'm curious to see what the others look like. Besides, Maddie seems downright terrified to wrangle them on her own.

"What, do you need a chaperone to face the big bad boys?" I tease her, rising to my feet, "Come on. I'll go with you."

Resigned, Maddie trails me out the back door onto the patio. The night is warm and breezy, and dusk gathers quickly as the sun plummets toward the horizon.

"I still haven't met the younger guys," I say over my shoulder to Maddie, "They've been making themselves pretty damn scarce. Not that I have high hopes, having met Cash."

"Yeah," she chuckles nervously, "He seems like kind of a dick, right?"

"Total dick," I agree. "Pretty hot though."

"S-sorry?" Maddie stammers, running a hand through her long dark blonde bob. God, she can be such a puritan sometimes.

"What? He is," I shrug, "Did you see those tattoos? And that hair? God lord. It's like if Jon Snow and Thor had a super sexy, tatted-up love child. Not sure how that would work biologically, but—"

"I mean, yeah, he's pretty attractive…" Maddie allows slowly, "But I mean, he's kind of off limits, right? All the boys are. What with Mom and John's history and everything?"

I nearly stop in my tracks at Maddie's uncharacteristic leap of logic.

"Whoa, whoa. I wasn't planning on jumping him or anything, Maddie," I laugh, "Unless you think he'd be into it, that is."

I watch as Maddie's face goes perfectly still, her mouth hardening into a tight straight line. I hate to say it, but she's *always* been something of a prude, my big sister. I mean for god's sake, she's only had about three boyfriends in her entire life. And all of them were long, drawn out, monogamous relationships. I shudder at the very thought.

"Christ, Maddie. I'm kidding," I say, snapping my sister out of her dead-eyed trance.

"Oh. Right," she mutters, "I knew that."

"We need to get you drunk ASAP tonight," I laughs, "The rat race is turning you into something of a downer, my dear."

It's so weird that her mind would leap immediately to whether or not it's OK for us to hook up with John's sons. Maybe all that boring relationship sex is screwing with her straight-and-narrow sensibilities? I hadn't even considered that question myself. But, then again, I have someone waiting for me back at Sheridan. Someone who would surely put these rowdy country boys to shame.

I spot one such country boy standing at the end of the dock, looking out across the water. He's big and broad-shouldered like his dad, and tatted-up like Cash, but with much lighter ash-brown hair.

"Hey there," I call to him as Maddie and I approach.

He ignores me completely, keeping his gaze on the water.

"Maybe he didn't hear you?" Maddie suggests in a whisper.

Maybe he's just being a dick, I think to myself, marching right up to him.

"Hey," I repeat, tapping on his muscled shoulder, "What's up?"

I take a step back, startled, as he raises his hand to me. For a terrifying second, I'm reminded of the other night at the bar—the moment when that skinhead maniac cocked back his arm to pummel Danny into the ground. But no...this guy is simply trying to shut me up. Looks like he's just as charming as his big brother after all. What's so damn fascinating about the lake, anyway?

Following the younger son's gaze out across the water, I spot the source of his intense focus. Two built, barreling bodies are racing toward us, cutting the water with strong, sure strokes. I'm guessing that it's the two other brothers, having a little pre-dinner race. I'll never understand men and their need to make *everything* into a contest.

Taking a big step back to avoid getting drenched, I watch as the two men soar toward the dock, sending up a huge jet of water in their wake. Crossing my arms, I brace myself to meet the third of John's sons. Maybe he'll be more of a conversationalist than this cavemen brothers? But something tells me not to get my hopes up.

I look on as the swimmers grab hold of the wooden dock and pull themselves effortlessly up out of the water. Just as they climb side-by-side onto the planks and straighten up, the fiery orange sun blazes out from behind a cloud just above the horizon. I squint into the bright sunlight, blinded by the sudden burst. When my eyes start to adjust, I find myself starting at a pair of exceptionally cut torsos, dripping with lake water and absolutely perfect in shape and tone. I recognize Cash's tattoos at once, averting my attention to the other brother, whose tapered, muscular waist forms a perfect v. His fitted swim trunks hang dangerously low, and a dark trail of hair leads down from his navel, drawing my gaze to the impressive bulge announcing itself beneath his bathing suit. It's that tantalizing trail that snags my attention for its striking familiarity. And when I widen my focus and take this stranger in as a whole, that uncanniness only becomes more pronounced. Somewhere deep within the recesses of my mind, an alarm starts to wail. But why? As the blood red sun finally dips down below the horizon, my unblinded eyes flick up to the man's face.

For a split second, I convince myself that I must be hallucinating. I've had too much to drink. I'm crazed with cabin fever after one day in the woods. Surely, I can't *actually* be seeing what my mind would have me believe. But as the stranger's eyes lock squarely with mine, blazing like the finest of emeralds, there can be no mistaking him.

Luke Hawthorne stands at the end of the dock, staring at me with utter disbelief. My entire world tilts on its axis as I scramble to understand this turn of events. Luke is here. At the lake house. With John's sons. He is John's son. And if Luke is John's son—John, who my mother has been shacked up with for months doing god knows what— Then he and I... We're...

I bring my wine glass to my lips, taking a huge swig as time speeds back up to the present. My heart pounds wildly in my ears, obscuring the banter that flies in the air between the three brothers. I watch, paralyzed, as Luke gages my reaction. His expression goes from shocked, to curious, to something approaching happy surprise. Holy shit...is he going to tell all of our siblings that we know each other? He can't. They *can't* know. I can practically feel the panic light up my body like a neon sign, and it's not lost on Luke either. I watch as he realizes that I'm not going to acknowledge him. Watch as disappointment, then indifference take hold of his features. He tears his eyes away from me, playing it cool as ever. Unless he isn't playing at all—maybe he couldn't care less about finding me here. Me, the daughter of the woman who's been living with his Dad, and... And...

I watch as if from outside my own body as Luke shoots me a casual smile and strides right past me toward the house. Clutching onto my wine glass like a life preserver, I hurry to avert my eyes, totally at a loss. What's the proper etiquette for the moment you figure out that the guy you want to bone is related to your Mom's fuck buddy?

Dear god. I'm going to need a refill before I even *begin* to deal with this one.

Chapter Six

Well, it's official, I think to myself as I sink even further down into my seat at the kitchen table, *I can now say in all truth that I know what hell looks like.*

I barely hear a word of the conversation buzzing in the air as the Porter and Hawthorne families tuck into their dinners. Unable to even think about touching my own food, I sip my wine in shell-shocked silence. How can this be happening? How can it be possible that Luke freaking Hawthorne is sitting across from me at "family dinner", looking calm and collected as ever? Is he not the least bit freaked out to see me here? Does he care at all that our relationship has just gotten ten times weirder, perhaps even impossible, given our parents' history? How am I the only one who's freaking out about this whole goddamn side show?

"So nice to have everyone here at last," my Mom trills, looking around at the seven less-than-enthusiastic faces around the table. "Have all you kids gotten to know each other by now?"

I can feel Luke's eyes boring into me from across the table. He's waiting for me to explain how it is we know each other. Waiting to see if I've changed my mind. If I could swan dive into my wine glass right now, I would.

"More or less," Cash replies to my mom.

"Glad you kids are all acquainted," John says curtly.

"Your dad is a man of few words," Mom smiles at John, "Are all you boys strong silent types as well?"

"I don't know if I'd put it that way," Luke puts in, his voice impossibly even. "We all have more than our fair share of differences."

"Sounds like my girls, too," Mom says, "Annabel takes after me, with her photography and all. Maddie's our little working girl over in Seattle. And Sophia's studying drama and dance at Sheridan University."

"Yeah, I know," Luke replies, his green eyes gleaming with grim determination as they swing back to my face.

I send a huge gulp of wine gushing down the wrong pipe, and double over as a coughing fit overtakes me. So much for playing it cool. What the hell does Luke think he's doing? He can't possibly think that sharing our backstory is a good idea, here? Our families' small talk is drowned out by the frantic thundering of my heart. I glance desperately up at Luke the second I stop choking, looking at him directly for the first time since he sprung up out of that lake like some kind of water god. Maybe I can master ESP in the next two minutes and beg him not to say another word? But there's no need for ESP with him. He can read people like open books. It helps that the look I'm giving him clearly reads, "NO. PLEASE. DON'T." in gigantic bold print.

"So, you and Sophie are at the same school?" Maddie says to Luke, dragging my mind back to the present, "I'm sure undergrads and graduate students don't see much of each other, though."

"Oh, I think Sophie and I have seen each other around school once or twice," Luke replies, his strong square jaw pulsing with the tension of words unsaid. Finally, my icy panic has a second to thaw. Maybe he's not going to blow our spot just yet...

"Sophie, you didn't tell me you knew Luke!" Mom gasps, turning to me with a rapturous smile.

"Well, I didn't exactly know we were family friends," I snap before I can stop myself, "Or that I'd be seeing him—them—here, did I? Besides, I don't know him. We just go to the same school. With thousands of other people. It's not the same thing."

A crease appears between Luke's perfectly sculpted brows as I blush furiously. He's gone from frustrated to downright pissed. I don't know why I'm lying about how we know each other, I'm purely in survival mode, here.

"I guess Sheridan is a much bigger school than the one me and John met in," Mom goes on, totally oblivious to the drama unfolding between me and Luke. "Little Flathead County High was not exactly a hopping place. What did we have, a hundred kids per class?"

"We still had our fun though, didn't we?" John says, grinning suggestively at Mom.

"We sure did," Mom smiles back, looking for the world like a blushing schoolgirl. What the hell is this, now?

"So, what, you two dated in high school or something?" Annabel asks, finally putting voice to the subject that all us adult children have been skirting around.

"Or something…" John mutters.

"Actually," Mom says breathlessly, "John and I were engaged."

My stomach turns over as I whip around to face my mother—and I'm not the only person at the table looking suddenly nauseated. My sisters, Luke, Cash, and their youngest brother Finn are all staring at our parents with rapt, uneasy focus.

"Well, that's a conversation we haven't had," Maddie says curtly, glaring at our mother.

"You were engaged?" I splutter, "What…When?!"

"All through senior year of high school," Mom tells us, sighing nostalgically.

"But I couldn't keep this one pinned down in Podunk, Montana," John adds, none-too-amiably.

"My scholarship to art school came through, and I couldn't pass it up," Mom shrugs, "Besides, we were so young…"

"Isn't art school where you met Dad?" Anna asks our mother.

"It is," Mom allows. A shadow crosses over her face as Dad comes up for the first time since we've been here.

"So if that scholarship hadn't come through, you would have stayed here and married John..." Anna goes on, a dreamy look in her eye. I wish to god that she would stop with these hypotheticals before I puke all over the table.

"That was the plan," John says, sneaking a warm glance at our mother.

"So if you think about it," Anna goes on, "John is sort of, like, our almost-dad."

There it is. The exact thing I was trying not to think this whole time. Even if we had no knowledge of our parents' past, Luke and I have still shared this baffling connection the whole time we've known each other— when I was crushing on him during his lectures, when we shared that steamy hookup in the bathroom of the bar, when we stayed up all last night texting each other the dirtiest things we could think of... Our entire relationship is suspect, now. And there's nothing we can do about it.

"Almost-dad," Mom laughs, "What a thing to say, Anna! You've always been the inventive one."

"She's got a point though," John says with a shrug, "There's no way of knowing what might have been, if only..."

"No real need to wonder about what might have been though, is there?" Maddie snaps, her face reddening, "Seeing as we had a dad, and all. A great dad."

"Maddie," I say softly, trying to reach her through her simmering rage.

"Had a dad?" asks Finn, the youngest Hawthorne brother.

"Yeah. Had. He died," Maddie all but spits, "But I guess someone forgot to relay that information, too."

I fix my gaze on the table, blinking back sudden tears. I can feel Luke's green eyes hard on my face, but I don't dare meet them. The empathy I know I'd find there would put me right over the edge. And I won't give anyone here the satisfaction of making me cry.

"Excuse me," Maddie mutters, "I just…I don't seem to have much of an appetite."

She leaps up from the table in a huff, effectively ending this bizarro family dinner. As the group begins to disperse, all I can think of is getting Luke alone. Not for our previously planned liaison, but to regroup and figure out what the hell we're going to do now. I finally raise my eyes to his over the table as our families scatter with a look that clearly says, *We need to talk.*

Luke jerks his head subtly toward the patio door, and I nod my assent. Amid the chaos of the broken-up dinner party, we slip away to reconvene in a less public arena.

Dewy blades of grass cling to my bare ankles as I hurry across the wide backyard of the Hawthorne lake house, trailing Luke down to the dock. My head swims with new gleaned information and, to be perfectly honest, a bit more wine than may have been wise. But hey, something tells me that this is a conversation I'll be happy to be a bit buzzed for.

Luke's broad, built figure stands out against the inky lake, imposing and flawless as ever. It's still bizarre to see him in shorts and a tee shirt, rather than slacks and a button down. I actually find myself wishing we could be back in that lecture hall together. Economic theory may have bored me to tears, but at least our dynamic was clear cut then. But now? The status of our relationship couldn't be any murkier.

"Well," Luke remarks gruffly, looking up as I approach the end of the dock, "Fancy meeting you here."

It's the first full sentence he's spoken to me since he nearly gave me a heart attack climbing out of that lake.

"No shit, Prof," I mutter back, crossing my arms as the cool breeze chills my bare skin.

"So," he goes on, shoving a hand through his short chestnut hair, "Do you want to tell me why the hell you lied to our families back there?"

"I'm...Sorry?" I breathe, gaping up at him.

"Why did you tell them we didn't know each other?" he demands, "That's just going to fuck this up even more."

"What the hell did you expect me to say?!" I laugh incredulously, "'Luke was technically my teacher, but that didn't stop us from trying to do the nasty anyway. Oh, and I spent all of last night jerking myself off in the guest room as he described exactly how he'd fuck me when he got the chance?' Is that what you had in mind?"

"Of course not," he snaps, "Don't play dumb with me. I know you too well for that. We could have spun things our way without giving all the dirty details. But hey, if you'd rather pretend we've never met and just go our separate ways, then—"

"That's not what I want at all," I cut him off emphatically, "That's the last thing in the world I want, Luke."

"You have a funny way of showing it," he replies, cocking an eyebrow at me.

"Come *on*," I cry, exasperated. "I just found out that you're practically related to me all of two hours ago. I'm still trying to figure out—"

"What is there to figure out?" he growls, taking a step toward me, "Why should it matter that our parents know each other?"

"They don't just know each other," I breathe, my body heating up despite myself as he closes the space between us, "They're living together. They were engaged, for fuck's sake. How the hell is none of this freaking you out?"

"Because it doesn't matter, Sophie," he says fiercely, grabbing me by the hips, "All the matters is how we feel about each other. We're not doing anything wrong."

"I don't—I mean…" I gasp, laying my hands on the firm panes of his chest.

"Look, in the end, I don't give a shit how we play this with our families," he goes on, circling my waist with his powerful arms, "We can pretend we don't know each other. We can ignore each other completely when they're around. Whatever you like. But I *won't* pretend that I don't still want you, Sophie. I couldn't, even if I tried."

"I don't think I could either," I whisper, turning my face to his, "Luke, I don't want this thing between us to be over yet."

"Then don't end it," he rasps, running a hand through my long caramel locks. I gasp as his fingers close tightly, tugging my hair with just the right amount of force. Just the way he promised last night…

"How can you go from professor, to perfect son, to *this* in the blink of an eye?" I ask him breathlessly, lifting my face to his.

"You're not the only one with acting practice, I guess," he grins, pulling my body flush against his, "Do you have any idea how hard it was to act like I wasn't thrilled to see you here earlier?"

"What? Why thrilled?" I ask, baffled.

"Because I thought I'd have to wait two whole weeks to get my hands on you again," he tells me, running those hands down along my back, "But now…"

A shudder runs down my spine as Luke grabs hold of my firm ass, tugging me hard against him. I gasp as I feel his hard cock pressed urgently against my thigh. Circling his broad shoulders with trembling arms, I look up at him in the gathering twilight.

"I'm really going to need you to kiss me now, Luke," I whisper.

Without another word, he brings his mouth to mine. I melt against his perfectly balanced body, grinding my hips against his insistent desire. He works my mouth open, sweeping his expert tongue against mine. The smoky, sweet taste of him gets me drunker in a moment than I've felt all evening. It's all I can do to keep from tearing his clothes off right here on the dock.

We may be resolved to see this thing through, despite our families' tangled history...but something tells me that giving them a front row seat to us *getting down and dirty* would still be ill-advised, to say the least.

Though Luke and I manage to pull ourselves away from each other before things get out of hand that night, we do leave the dock with some ground rules in place. First, we decide that it's best to keep our families in the dark about the details of our acquaintance for now. All they need to know is that we met at Sheridan. That's it. Seeing as neither of our families are particularly forthcoming about their emotional and personal lives, it won't be out of character for us to keep our lips sealed.

Secondly, we agree to keep our distance for the next couple of weeks, at least when other members of our families are around. We can sneak off together and get up to anything we like, but when the others are watching, we'll keep our hands to ourselves. We'll be back at Sheridan in two weeks' time, anyway. Surely we can control ourselves until then. Any interference from our families now will just jeopardize this thing between us...whatever "this thing" might turn out to be.

"If I know my dad at all," Luke says, as we walk back to the house after our long conversation, "This little fling isn't going to last forever."

"Not with my mom, it's not," I laugh, "Since my dad died, she's barely kept a guy around for two weeks running. Whatever's going on between her and John will be kaput by the time summer is out."

"We'll just be patient then," Luke smiles, taking my hand in his. We've paused in the shadow of the enormous lake house, hidden from sight. "Trust me. It'll be well worth the wait."

"Oh, I trust you," I breathe, giving his hand a squeeze. "I'll be counting down the days."

"This trip will be over before you know it," he murmurs, tucking a lock of hair behind my ear, "Who knows? We might even think it's funny. Someday."

"That might be overstating things," I mutter.

"Fair point," he allows, lifting my chin with two strong fingers. His smile fades as he looks down at me in the moonlight, green eyes gleaming. "I have to say, Sophie. You impress me."

"Impress you?" I breathe, "How—?"

"It's not just anyone who could roll with the punches like this," he goes on, trailing those fingers down my throat, "I like a woman with an open mind."

"Oh yeah?" I smile, taking a step toward him, "What *else* are you hoping I'll be open to?"

"You'll see," he grins back, bringing his mouth swiftly to mine. He lays one firm, final kiss on my lips before breaking away. "See you, Sophie. Try not to stay up all night thinking about me."

"Your modesty is truly stunning," I shoot back, rolling my eyes as Luke turns and walks away from me into the lake house.

He's not wrong, though. I doubt I'll sleep a wink tonight, knowing that Luke Hawthorne is under the same roof as me. It's a good thing our ground rules for this trip have some wiggle room. Now all I have to do is figure out how to get some privacy with my ardent paramour. I look out across the expansive lake, the sprawling forests, the acres of open space without a soul to be found...

Who knows? Perhaps privacy won't be so hard to come by after all.

Chapter Seven

I've got to hand it to Luke, he really isn't a shabby actor. As the days goes by, I'm frankly stunned by how easy it is to hide the true nature of our relationship from our families. Any time we're in the presence of our siblings or parents, we give Oscar-worthy performances of not having any interest in each other. It almost becomes like a game for us... If I'm honest, I think it's kind of hot, having a secret like this. It certainly adds to the anticipation as we wait for the perfect moment to sneak away together.

A couple nights into the trip, the eight of us attempt another big family meal. Amazingly enough, not a single tear is shed from appetizers to dessert. Tensions have died down remarkably fast around here. I guess we're all a lot more adaptable than we give ourselves credit for. Even Maddie, who was so upset the first night that I thought for sure she was going to leave, seems much calmer. Come to think of it, she seems calmer—and happier—than I've seen her in years. Maybe all this lake air is doing her good?

I'm standing at the kitchen sink, rinsing off plates and stacking them in the dishwasher. As the rest of the family disperses, I feel a thrill as Luke strides over to me, leaning against the kitchen counter. My spine straightens under his intent stare, and I peer around to make sure no one's watching us.

"Stay in character, Hawthorne," I murmur, keeping my eyes on the sink.

"Don't worry," he smiles, "I'm a pro, remember? I just wanted to see what your plans were for tomorrow morning."

"Oh…Uh…I don't really have any," I tell him, "Why?"

"I thought you might be interested in coming out for a run with me," he says, casually crossing his arms.

"Is that some kind of a euphemism?" I whisper conspiratorially.

"Maybe," he grins.

"Well then…sure," I say, excitement rising in my belly, "I'd love to go out for a run with you. I need a little exercise."

"Great," he says, thumping his fist on the counter, "I'll see you at 5a.m."

I promptly drop the plate I'm holding into the sudsy sink.

"5 a.m.?!" I splutter, "What are you, some kind of masochist?"

"Come on, Soph," he grins at me, "Aren't you dancer types supposed to be made out of steel or something? This should be nothing for you."

"Made out of steel, maybe. But also *very* fond of sleeping in," I mutter.

"Hey, if you don't want to…" Luke shrugs.

"Ugh. Fine," I sigh, "See you bright and early, *bro*."

That gets to him. I laugh as his face twists uneasily at my address. Before he can reply, his brothers appear in the kitchen behind us.

"Cash and I are going into town for a few rounds at the Pourhouse," Finn says to Luke. "You wanna come with?"

"Always," Luke replies, turning away from me without another glance.

I return to the task at hand as the boys file out, suppressing a smile as I imagine what Luke has in store for me tomorrow morning.

***

Though I balked at the idea of rising before the crack of dawn, my eyes fly open before my alarm even goes off. This is the first time Luke and I are stealing away on our own, after all—it may as well be Christmas morning. I roll out of bed and dig through my backpack, pulling out my most flattering workout clothes and throwing them on at lightning speed. Mornings here at the lake are pretty cool, so I slip into black leggings, a strappy sports bra, and a lightweight pullover. By the time I'm lacing up my favorite kicks, it's 5a.m. Time to go rouse my "running buddy".

I pad through the slumbering house, trying my best not to wake anyone as I approach Luke's bedroom door. My entire body is awake with anticipation, energized and ready for him, whatever he has in store for me. Taking a deep, steadying breath, I stop outside Luke's door and raise my first to give it a light rap. But before I can knock, the door swings open. Luke appears in the doorway wearing nothing but running shorts and a small backpack. His sculpted chest and arms are completely bare, and I can't help but trail my gaze all along his cut torso. The sudden, powerful urge to tackle him back into his room and onto the bed nearly overwhelms me.

"There you are," he grins, "Come on. Let's go."

As he passes me, I see that his well-loved running shoes are already laced up. For the first time, it occurs to me that Luke was a star athlete at Sheridan as an undergrad. Particularly when it came to track and field. His specialty, if I recall correctly, was long-distance running. Oh god…what have I gotten myself into?

"Luke," I whisper, following him down the stairs, "Are we…actually going for a run?"

"Of course," he replies, glancing over his shoulder at me, "What did you think?"

"Oh, nothing," I mutter, feeling my excitement slam into a brick wall.

We make our way out into the crisp morning, stepping onto the wide verandah. I have to admit, I don't mind seeing this place so early in the day. The quiet that envelops us is unlike anything I've ever experienced before.

"OK," Luke says, moving through a series of light stretches, "I'll take you out on my usual path. Five miles good for you?"

I can already feel my muscles tightening in protest. Though I'm no stranger to cardio, I'm much more of a yoga girl myself when left to my own devices. But there's no way I'm backing down from this outing now.

"Sure," I say to Luke, giving my shoulders a roll. "Sounds great."

"Cool," he smiles, taking the porch steps two at a time, "I'll take the lead."

I watch as he sets off down the driveway, his muscles working together in perfect unison. Hurrying to follow, I let a wry smile play across my face. If only my movement teacher Gary could see me now, huh?

Despite my reservations about this little excursion, my body is thrilled to get a bit of exertion. My lungs fill gratefully with cool mountain air as I dash along in Luke's wake. His form is perfect as he leads me along back roads through the dense forest. With every long stride he takes, the muscles of his back and shoulders ripple deliciously beneath his tanned skin. His calves are cut to perfection, and his ass is positively rock hard. If his gorgeous form could always be my view while running, I'd be a marathoner in no time.

Little by little, we ascend up toward the tree line. A runner's high washes over me as we climb, and I forget that there's anyone else in the world besides Luke and me.

I lose track of the time, the miles, and the effort it takes to keep up with my all-star companion. I'm just happy for this moment out of time with him—away from our families, our school, everything. And just when I think this morning couldn't get any lovelier, the thick forest around us suddenly gives way to open space. We've reached the summit. My breath catches in my throat as I skid to a halt behind Luke, who's come to a sudden stop.

"What do you think?" he grins breathlessly, sweeping out his glistening arms.

I look past him at the rolling landscape, struck dumb by the gorgeous view. We've stepped out into a wide clearing overlooking the turquoise lake and surrounding woods. A brilliant sky arches overhead, run through with streaks of pink and orange clouds. A cool breeze brushes deliciously against my flushed skin as I try and take in all this beauty at once.

"…Wow," I breathe. It's all I can manage.

"Worth the run?" Luke asks, slipping an arm around my waist.

"Well worth it," I smile up at him. "Thank you, Luke."

"Just wait," he grins, shucking off his lightweight backpack, "There's more."

I look on as he unzips the pack, producing a gigantic thermos of coffee and two tin mugs. A laugh escapes my throat as he hands the warm thermos to me.

"How did you know the way to my heart was massive amounts of coffee?" I smile.

"Lucky guess," he replies, sitting down on a wide, smooth rock overlooking the view.

I hand the thermos back to Luke, who pours out two steaming mugs of coffee. Warmed up by our trek, I shuck off my pullover and set it down on the rock beside him. I raise my arms above my head, shaking out my long locks and soaking in the early morning sun. I can feel Luke's gaze on my lithe body, lingering on my taut, bare stomach, the rise of my ass beneath my leggings. I've met plenty of guys who have liked me for my body before, but never one who looked at it so worshipfully, as Luke does. And never one who appreciated my mind just as much, for that matter.

"This is just about perfect," I say softly, in awe as the sun breaks over the hilly horizon.

"Yeah," he murmurs, drinking in the sight of me, "It is."

I almost feel bashful at the intensity of his admiration. Maybe I still can't believe that this amazing, complicated, fascinating person is interested in me at all. I've always had trouble taking people at their word, trusting them to step up and be there for me. But I'd happily be proven wrong, if I could just keep easing my guard down for Luke Hawthorne. It still has a ways to go, but hey—anything is possible, right?

Luke hands me a mug of coffee as I sit beside him on the flat rock, and I happily accept. Our bare shoulders touch as we sit side-by-side, nursing our black coffee as we look out across the expansive forested landscape.

"So," I say, giving him a playful nudge with my shoulder, "Is this where you used to bring all the local girls when you wanted to score?"

He lets out a bark of laughter, laying a hand on my knee as he replies, "It would have been, if any other girl could keep up with me. You're not as dreadful a runner as you led me to believe."

"You say the sweetest things," I drawl sarcastically.

"You love it," he teases, edging his hand ever-so-slightly up my thigh. My back arches as a shot of desire races up my spine. "But for real, Sophie," he goes on, "You are the first and only girl I've ever brought up here."

"Really?" I ask, softly, leaning against him as he runs his hand along my thigh.

"Really," he replies, turning his face toward mine. "I didn't have a lot of time for girls, back when I was a kid—collegiate escapades notwithstanding."

"All those hometown girls must have been heartbroken," I laugh. "But what do you mean, you didn't have time?"

Luke pauses for a long moment, his hand stilling on my leg as he sips his coffee. I can tell we're leaving his conversational comfort zone. I've never heard him mention his past before. I wonder how often he talks about that time in his life to anyone, even his family?

"Let's just say that there was a lot of slack to pick up around here, back then," he finally allows.

"I see... And who was the one slacking off?" I ask, seizing the opportunity to learn more about Luke's shadowy past.

He gives a gruff laugh, rubbing his sharp, stubble-studded jaw.

"The real question is, who *wasn't*?" he replies. "I guess my mom was the original slacker. She bailed on us before my brothers and I were in the double digits."

So *that's* what happened to Mrs. Hawthorne. I'd been too nervous to ask, up until now.

"She just left?" I press gently, laying my hand over Luke's.

"Yep," he sighs, "Decided she didn't want to 'rough it' out here in the woods with Dad anymore. Wanted the cosmopolitan life or whatever-the-fuck. We weren't living as well back then as we are now. Dad had only just started his construction firm, and things were tight. She just couldn't take it. Didn't have any faith that he could make it work. The funny thing is, business started picking up just after she bolted. Dad's company has been thriving ever since. This house here? That's what we was able to make for our family. That's what she missed out on."

"Where is she now?" I ask him, "Your mom."

"East coast," he says shortly, "Didn't waste any time starting a new family out there. Has a couple kids with her new husband and everything. We don't really hear from her much."

"Damn," I breathe, "That must have been so hard for you and your brothers."

"Not as hard as what you and your sisters have been through," he replies, his hard gaze softening, "I had no idea about your dad, before the other night..."

"How would you have known?" I shrug, taking a long sip of hot coffee, "It's not like we took each other's family histories before deciding to hook up."

"Yeah," he says with a small smile, "But I'm...I'm sorry you had to go through that, Sophie. That you're *going* through that. I know that kind of pain doesn't ever fully go away."

A hard knot starts to build in my throat. I've never talked about my Dad to anyone, besides my drama school classmates. But even then, it was only in terms of how his death was holding me back as a performer. The raw intensity of Luke's understanding is so new, so total, that it's almost overwhelming.

"You know. It's hard," I say vaguely, "But so are lots of things. Like growing up in a house full of dudes, I'd imagine."

"It could be...challenging," Luke laughs roughly, "Dad's not exactly what you'd call the 'nurturing type'. Most of his ideas about discipline involve a smack in the face, or worse. I was only seven when he became my only parent. Cash tried to shield me and Finn from the worst of it, but he and my dad butted heads so much that he was gone the second he turned eighteen. Didn't want anything more to do with us, so he went off and joined the army. Dad had always assumed that Cash would take over the business and everything, being the oldest. But, it became pretty clear, pretty fast, that it wasn't gonna happen like that."

"So it all fell to you..." I say softly.

"It all fell to me," he echoes, looking up at the brightening sky, "By the time I started high school, I was already carrying the weight my family's future on my shoulders. I was busting my ass to make straight A's, training like crazy to get myself a track scholarship, and working part time at my dad's firm to learn the ropes. He'd already decided that I was going to take over the business instead of Cash. I was only fifteen years old, but my whole life was already set in stone. Has been ever since."

"You never wanted any of it?" I go on, "Being the favorite son, the star athlete—"

"Well, being an athlete is the only thing that's kept me sane this whole time," he says wryly, "As long as I could take out my stress and anger on the field, or the track, I was good to go. If I had any choice in the matter, I'd probably be looking to get into personal training or physical therapy or something."

"But...You know you *do* have a choice, right Luke?" I ask. He turns to look at me, his square jaw clenched. "I'm sorry...I've said something wrong."

"No, it's fine. You're fine," he says, pulling me against his side, "It's just not as simple as all that, Sophie. I have certain responsibilities to my family, no matter what they've done in the past. He may have his flaws, but our Dad raised us all on his own. That's not nothing, you know? I think that's why I came down so hard on you about wanting to be a performer."

"When you kept me after class, you mean?" I ask. It's crazy to think that that happened only two weeks ago. It feels as though it's been years.

"Yeah," Luke says, running his hand along the dip of my waist, "I mean, there you were—showing up to my lecture every week, clearly the smartest person in the room, but hell bent on following your dreams instead doing something conventional with your life. You were so sure. So solid in what you believed in. Maybe I was just jealous of how free you seemed. It was shitty of me, trying to tell you how to live your life."

"I was kind of shitty," I mutter, a grin breaking across my face, "But I have a feeling you'll find a way to make it up to me."

Luke lets out a burst of laughter, and the heavy mood is dispelled at once. But as his hand comes to rest on my bare side, something else rushes in to fill the air around us. Something urgent and electric, something I've been holding at bay the whole time I've been here at the lake house.

"I definitely have a few ideas," Luke murmurs.

He takes the coffee mug out of my hand and sets it beside his on the ground. His hands are still warm from cradling the hot mug, and I shiver delightedly as those hands warm my breeze-chilled skin. Goosebumps fan out across my body as he runs his hands along my bare torso. I let my head fall back between my shoulders as he touches me, memorizing the shape of my body with his expert hands. A deep, pulsing pressure starts to build between my trembling legs, my breath coming harder and faster with each passing moment.

With his hard, green eyes fixed firmly on my glistening body, Luke eases me down onto the smooth slab of rock. Laying my body out before him, he swings his staggering form so that it's suspended above mine. I let my arms fall over my head as Luke lowers himself to me, holding up his massive form with two thickly muscled forearms. I moan softly as he catches my lips in his, savoring the sensation of our flushed, bare torsos meeting at last. That feeling of skin-on-skin is better than *anything*. My knees fall apart as Luke presses his hips to mine, letting me feel his long, throbbing erection as it rises in his running shorts. My back is pressed hard against the cool rock as I hook my ankles around Luke's hips, pulling his stiffening cock firmly against my sex.

He lets out a low, rumbling groan as I draw him closer, and kisses me hard along my throat. His stubble brushes against my skin as he moves down my neck, across my collarbone. Keeping his cock pressed hard against my aching sex, Luke pushes up my sports bra, letting my firm breasts spill out into the crisp morning air. I tug the garment up over my shoulders as he brings his lips hungrily to my breasts. I suck in a breath as he takes my hard nipple into his mouth, and cry out in surprised delight as he gives me a sharp bite there.

"Too much?" he rasps, glancing up at me with his smoldering green eyes.

"No," I gasp, digging my nails into his shoulders, "No, it's perfect."

"Good to know," he grins, closing his fingers around both of my erect nipples and pinching with just the right amount of force. Pain and pleasure flow like mad through my body, entwining dizzily. Looks like this star athlete isn't afraid to play a little rough.

I let my fingers rake over Luke's muscled back as he kisses down along my torso. My back arches as I feel his lips rove across my ribs, down my stomach, to the twin peaks of my hips bones. We kick off our sneakers as he nips at my hip, his hands running down along my slender thighs. My breath catches in my throat as he grabs the waist of my leggings and tugs them over the rise of my ass, down my legs. I pull myself onto my forearms as Luke kneels above me, raking his eyes all along my naked body. I'm sure he can see my heart pounding straight through my rib cage as I lie there before him, the cool breeze playing against my slick slit. I can certainly see *him* throbbing through the thin fabric of his running shorts—I'm surprised they haven't split open with the sheer enormity of his desire.

"Christ," Luke growls, running his hands up along my thighs, "I've been fucking *dying* to see you like this, Sophie."

My head spins as he pushes back against my knees, spreading me wide open right there before his eyes. I fall back against the smooth stone as he brings his lips to my inner thigh, kissing along my flushed skin. Burying my fingers in his cropped brown hair, I try and steady my racing heart as his mouth moves closer and closer to my pulsing, eager sex. His breath is warm against my wetness as he positions his massive body between my spread legs.

"Keep going," I tell him breathlessly.

"Damn. Already begging?" he grins, flicking his green eyes up to mine.

"If that's what you want," I whisper urgently.

"Go ahead then," he urges, his lips hovering mere inches from my sex, "Beg me."

"Please touch me, Luke," I plead as I writhe with want of him, "I want to feel your mouth on my pussy. I want to—"

But my words trail off into a wordless moan as Luke lays two strong fingers against my slit.

"Fuck, you're so wet…" he growls, stroking along the length of me.

"No shit," I laugh breathlessly.

I bite my lip to keep from screaming as he presses those fingers inside of me, letting me feel him right where I've wanted to for so long. He pulses his fingers against my soft flesh, sending low waves of sensation rumbling straight through my core. But just as those waves start to crest, I feel him push back the hood of my clit, exposing that hard, throbbing button to his expert touch. As he drives his fingers firmly inside of me, I feel his tongue glance against that bundle of nerves. The steadily building sensation rising in my core peaks with a strong rush of pleasure. Delicious warmth surges through my body as Luke flicks the tip of his tongue against my clit, tracing firm circles as his fingers collide with that tender place inside of me.

"Luke," I gasp, holding onto his shoulders for dear life, "I'm so close…"

"Just wait," he growls, his lips vibrating against my sex as his voice rasps with need.

I cry out in surprise as Luke grabs me by the hips and swings me up into his arms. I keep my legs wrapped firmly around his waist, supporting my own weight as he spins me around, tugging down his running shorts with one hand. I laugh breathlessly as he holds me effortlessly suspended, reaching into his backpack and grabbing a condom.

"Someone thought ahead," I grin, nipping at his ear.

"I may not be much of a boy scout," he smiles, ripping open the wrapper with his teeth, "But I *am* always prepared…"

Our mouths meet ravenously as he sits on the smooth surface of the rock and rolls the condom down his cock. I shiver with delight as I taste myself on his lips, his tongue. Finally, he begins to lower me down onto his lap, and I feel the swollen tip of his cock pressing against my throbbing, soaking wet slit. Hooking my ankles behind his back, I let my mouth fall open as he eases me down along his rock hard length. I take his cock inside of me inch by glorious inch, groaning as I feel him fill me like no man ever has.

"Jesus, Sophie…" he growls, circling my waist with one strong arm, "You feel so good wrapped around my cock."

"You have no idea," I whisper, clasping my hands behind his neck.

Slowly, we start to move together, our hips bucking with deliberate, forceful strokes. His cock drives up inside of me, faster and harder with every pass. I've never had a man this big before, never felt someone open me so deeply. I can feel him colliding with the core of me, splitting me open as I bounce on his lap in a state of blissful wonder. I let my head fall back, taking in the brightening sky arching overhead. That is, until Luke's fingers find their way back to my clit. Then, the whole world sets to spinning madly around me.

"Goddammit," I moan, bucking madly on Luke's gigantic, pummeling manhood, "Goddammit, that's so good…"

"I'm close babe," he growls through gritted teeth, bearing down on my hard, throbbing clit. "I'm right there…"

"I want to come with you," I gasp back, locking eyes with him as his full lips part.

He keeps his fingers pressed firmly to that tender button as he rears back and pounds into me with more force than I could imagine possible, his massive cock driving straight into the very center of me. That deep, leveling stroke sends me soaring over the edge into dizzying bliss. As I feel him come deep inside of me, his cock pulsing like mad as he lets go, a rolling wave of sensation crashes through my body. The feeling sweeps across my every frayed nerve, infusing each and every one of my cells with searing heat. I'm run through with the restorative, unimaginable joy of true satisfaction—a feeling I've never shared with another person…until now.

I collapse forward against Luke's unbending form, feeling his heart beating wildly against mine. For a long while, it's all we can do to try and catch our breath as we stay here, tangled up in each other's arms beneath the clear, breaking day. At long last, I manage to sit back on his lap, training my eyes on his. Not a single word comes to mind that could encapsulate what I just felt with him…but when those green eyes lock with mine, I see that no words are needed. We both know exactly what we shared, here.

Gently, Luke helps me to my feet, cleaning himself up with a towel he was wise enough to pack as I slip back into my leggings. My sex is already sore and satisfied as I straighten up, my breasts bouncing freely as I watch Luke step back into his shorts. He turns to face me across the clearing, looking as at ease as I've ever seen him. With a slow smile, he opens his arms to me. I rush forward, closing the space between us as I wrap my arms around his waist. Resting my cheek against the hard pane of his chest, I look out over the wide world, wondering how the hell I got to be so lucky.

And that's when I hear it—a branch snapping off in the woods.

Luke and I whip around to face each other, eyes going wide. When the first sound gives way to another—most definitely the sound of someone or something approaching—we lurch away from each other's arms. Heart in my throat, I rush to pull on my bra and sweatshirt while Luke slips back into his sneakers, sitting down on the rock that just served us so well. He picks up a coffee mug and thrusts one in my hand as I hop on over toward him, nearly face-planting as my shoelaces tangle beneath me. I plop down beside him, wrangling my face into a casual expression as those footsteps close in on our clearing. It's then that my ears pick up a second sound. Something softer, crisper, absolutely distinct.

The sound of a camera shutter.

"Oh, hey you guys," I hear my younger sister say from behind us.

Luke and I turn to see Annabel stepping into the clearing, her DSLR camera slung around her neck. Relief and frustration war for control of my mind. On the one hand, thank god she didn't happen along five minutes sooner. On the other, how can it be this hard to get a second alone with Luke?

"Hey Anna," Luke says calmly, "You're up early."

"So are you," she observes, looking between me and Luke as if trying to solve a puzzle.

"We were out for a run," I tell her evenly, holding up a sneaker-clad foot for her to see, "Gotta work off all the meat and potatoes Mom keeps making, right?"

"Mhm," Anna replies, raising her camera to capture the view unfolding before us. Her response is hard to read. Do I detect something crackling beneath her composure? Something that sounds very much like disapproval? Maybe I'm being paranoid... I just can't be sure.

Luke and I steal a glance at each other while Anna's distracted by the view. Neither of us can believe how close a call this was. We'll have to get even more creative with our clandestine meetings in the future, because god knows this can't be the last time that we have each other. Not now that we know exactly how good it can be.

"Well, I'm probably gonna head back," Luke says, standing to go. He packs up the thermos and mugs, swinging the bag onto his back.

"I might just walk back with Anna," I tell him, "If that's cool with her, I mean."

"Sure," Anna says, totally absorbed by the world she sees through her lens.

"See you back there," Luke says to me, his eyes lingering on my face. I can feel the longing rising off of him like steam. How nice it would be, to take our time together. To stay here, unhurried, and explore each other's bodies all day.

All in good time, I try and tell him with my eyes.

"See you later," I say instead, crossing my arms tightly.

Luke turns to go without another word, taking off at a jog along the path we traversed to get here. I turn away from him, marveling at how relaxed my body feels. That uphill run was totally worth it, that's for damn sure.

My dreamy daze is punctured as a flash of color catches my eye on the ground at my feet. Lying beside the rock that Luke and I just put to good use is a bright yellow condom wrapper. My stomach flips over as the sight registers in my sex-addled mind, just as Anna is swinging her camera my way. I jerk my body across the rock, planting my foot firmly over the wrapper and grinding it into the dirt. Aiming my best Hollywood smile at Anna's lens, I spread my arms wide in a ridiculous pose.

"I'm ready for my close-up," I grin, mugging every which way and effectively ruining her shot.

"You're such a ham," she mutters, lowering her camera and striding away from me. "What are you, already withdrawing from the spotlight after one week away from acting school?"

"You know me," I laugh, "Always the attention hog. Middle child syndrome. You understand."

I quickly bury the condom wrapper while her back is turned, spooked by the close call. If Luke and I are going to make it through the next couple of weeks without being found out, we're gonna need to step up our discretion game. Especially around Anna. My younger sister is one of the most observant people I know. Maddie and my mom will each be too wrapped up in their own shit to notice if I steal off with John's gorgeous son time and again, but Anna could very well catch on if we're not more careful.

Part of me wonders if I should just confide in her right off the bat. I already let it slip that I had a thing for one of my TA's at Sheridan. What if she puts the pieces together? It'll be much worse if she finds me out, rather than being told up front. But how can I know that she won't be totally weirded out by my relationship with

Luke? What if she tells me that it's sick, or wrong, or just depressing to be screwing him while our parents are…whatever our parents are? I couldn't stand that. I trust Anna's opinion more than anyone's. So if she disapproved of me and Luke…I don't know how I'd get over that. I'm not willing to risk it. Not just yet.

"Are you coming?" Anna says over her shoulder, moving back off into the woods, "I want to get some more shots before I lose this light."

"Right. Sure. I'm coming," I call after her, standing to follow. Better to keep my secret to myself for the time being, I decide. After all, what's a little lie of omission between sisters?

Nice try, I think to myself, following in Anna's path. Great. Even my own subconscious can't be convinced that I'm doing the right thing, here. But how could something this wrong feel so, so right?

Chapter Eight

My newly whetted appetite for Luke trumps any reservations I might be having about keeping our relationship from Annabel and Madeleine. I'll tell them eventually, if and when the time is right...Meaning, once Mom has ditched John for her next conquest. He can't have much time left in my mother's good graces. She's been here at the lake house for weeks, after all. The clock must be running down on their little love affair.

Really though, I don't have much room in my mind for Mom, John, or any of the others. Luke has captivated me, mind and body...and heart too, if I'm being honest. We haven't said a word to each other about any sort of future beyond this summer, or made any attempt to label what it is we are to each other. None of that really seems to matter, with him. What's important is the deep understanding that's formed between us. The unheard-of degree of respect and admiration that we have for each other. That's more important than labels and titles any day.

As the days go by at the lake house, Luke and I get better and better at covering our tracks. We take separate routes to every rendezvous we plan, making sure that there's no way anyone else could stumble upon us. When we spend time with our siblings, we put on a great show of being neutral acquaintances. It's not that hard to sneak off whenever we wish—all eight of the Porters and Hawthornes have fallen into their own routines, here at the lake house. Neither of our families are particularly warm and cuddly—a fact that only makes it easier to peel off from the pack.

But while I'm intent on obscuring my relationship with Luke from my mom and sisters, there's one person I simply can't hold back from. My best friend, Danny.

"Are you fucking kidding me?!" he all but screams when I give him the skinny over the phone, late one night. "Professor Sexy Pants is, like, your step-brother?!?"

"No, no, *no*," I groan, flopping onto my twin bed, "Our parents aren't married. I mean, they *almost* were. Once. But it's totally not the same thing."

"Uh-huh," Danny drawls, "Sure. Whatever you have to tell yourself."

"You don't think I'm some kind of freak, do you?" I ask him nervously.

"Only in the best sense of the word, my darling," he assures me, "And remember, that's high praise in my book."

"Gee. Thanks," I mumble.

"I mean it!" he gushes, "I saw *Cruel Intentions*. I know a thing or two about stepbrother bangin'."

"Well, since you're the expert, maybe you can tell me how the hell I'm going to break it to my family, down the line?" I suggest.

"Is there going to *be* a down the line?" Danny asks, surprised, "I thought this was a summer fling sort of situation."

"I mean…it's hard to say," I waffle. "You never know what the future—"

"Oh. My. God," Danny cuts me off, "Sophia Elizabeth Porter, are you falling for this guy?"

"Uh-oh, you're using my middle name. Does that mean I'm in trouble?" I laugh.

"Don't change the subject. Do you really like him or what?" Danny demands.

"I don't…I mean…Maybe?" I sigh, "He's not like anyone I've ever been with."

"In that he has a personality and is not a major douche-rocket?" Danny replies.

"Nice."

"The truth hurts, hun," he goes on, "Look, I'm thrilled that you've found someone who gets that screwed up little brain of yours. It doesn't hurt one bit that he's gorgeous, and brilliant, and a bit kinky from the sound of it. Just do me a favor while you're out there screwing brother dearest in the woods, would you?"

"Of course. Anything for you," I say dryly.

"Don't go falling so deeply for him that you can't pull yourself out of it in a pinch, OK?" Danny warns me.

"I thought you were all for him?" I ask, surprised.

"Oh, I am," Danny assures me, "After his knight in shining armor moment at The Bear Trap, I'm a huge Luke Hawthorne fan. But there's a soft, gooey heart underneath all that armor of *yours*, Sophie. Don't let down all your defenses at once. At least not until you know exactly what you're up against."

I assure my best friend that I'll be careful. But even as I'm swearing up and down to keep myself from getting in too deep with Luke, I realize that restraint is the last thing I want with him. My feelings for Luke pull at me like a strong current. I'd have to fight like hell to beat against that force. Wouldn't it be easier to give into the tug? Let myself be carried away?

Or would that just be a surefire way to drown?

***

Part of keeping my relationship with Luke on the DL is making sure to spend time with the rest of the Porters and Hawthornes once in a while. Toward the end of my first week at the lake house, I decide to make good on some sister time and spend the afternoon with Maddie and Anna down on the dock. We're lounging around on the sun-warmed boards, bikini-clad and peaceful. They have no idea that my relaxed state is thanks, in large part, to a vigorous fucking from Luke in the bed of the family pickup truck early this morning. I have to cross my bare legs as a resounding pang of longing shoots up through my body at the mere memory of it. Hopefully, my gigantic black sunglasses obscure the furious flush that rises in my cheeks.

Maddie's quizzing Anna about taking a gap year before college when I manage to wrangle my attention back to the conversation at hand. My older sister sits with her feet in the water, a red bandana tying up her short dirty blonde hair. Anna lays on her stomach, letting the sun kiss her shoulders. I sit cross legged, slightly apart from them, absentmindedly fingering my mermaid tail braid as they chat.

"I give you a lot of credit," Maddie says, "I wouldn't have had the wherewithal to take a gap year before college at your age."

"Well, you knew what you wanted to go to school for," Anna replies, "I'm still feeling it out."

"I just couldn't wait to get out of the house," I cut in, "Don't get me wrong, I love my program at Sheridan. But more than anything, getting away from Mom was the priority."

"Yeah, well. Imagine being the only one in the house with her after Dad died," Anna says curtly, not even looking back at me as she speaks.

I catch Maddie's perplexed gaze and return it. Anna's been really short with both of us these past couple of days. I try not to psych myself out about it, but it's hard to hold my unease at bay.

"So, uh…have you given any thought to how you'll spend the year?" Maddie presses, trying to bypass the awkward silence.

"Mostly just building up my photography portfolio," Anna returns, "I want to get some more portraits and event photography."

"I could hire you for the next ReImaged party!" Maddie gushes. ReImaged is the Seattle-based PR agency that she works at. The company specializes in "event marketing". From what I gather, most of what they do is throw fancy parties for rich people. I never would have imagined my big sister ending up in a field like that. All her life, Maddie talked about becoming a literature professor like our father, Archie. But after he died, I think carrying on in his footsteps was too painful a prospect for her.

"Yeah, maybe," Anna tells Maddie, "I was thinking of heading in a less corporate direction, though. Finn's letting me tag along to his band's show tonight to take some shots of them, actually."

"Finn's in a band?!" I exclaim. That doesn't exactly jive with my understanding of the youngest Hawthorne son. That guy is a complete mystery to me.

"Yeah. He's the lead vocalist," Anna tells me.

"But I've barely heard a full sentence out of him," Maddie says.

"Yeah. I didn't realize he spoke in full sentences," I joke.

"Maybe that's because neither of you lets anyone else get a word in. Ever think of that?" Anna snaps at me, her blue eyes flaring dangerously.

"Whoa, Anna…" I breathe, taken aback by her ferocity, "That's a little harsh."

"Yeah, well. The truth can be a bitch," my younger sister shoots back, standing to make her exit.

"Did we do something wrong?" Maddie asks nervously, "You seem really pissed off at us."

Anna turns her frank, unapologetic gaze first on Maddie, then on me. "I just wish the two of you would think about someone besides yourselves once in a while."

"Anna, what are you talking about?" I ask her, fearing that I already know the answer.

"Come on," Anna says, sounding more disappointed than angry now, "You can't play dumb with me, you guys. I know you too well for that."

And with that, she turns and marches away from us. I try and tell myself that she could be upset about any number of things. Maybe she's annoyed about hearing the details of my and Maddie's lives, far away from Mom? Maybe she's sick of being cooped up in this lake house with a bunch of people she has almost nothing common with? Or maybe, I dare to consider, she's somehow figured out the truth. Maybe she knows about me and Luke after all. But no…if that were it, why would she be mad at Maddie, too?

"Do you have any idea what she's on about?" my older sister asks me.

"Nope," I lie, "No idea."

"Huh," Maddie muses, "You know Anna. Always the sensitive one. We should probably just let her go off and do her own thing. Close quarters do weird things to people…"

That must be it. Just a case of cabin fever. Still, it wouldn't hurt to check up on my little sister later tonight, once she's cooled off a bit. The last thing I want is to let this toxic tension between us keep on mounting.

My thoughts are derailed as a flurry of motion catches my eye on the lake house lawn. A bright red kayak is being carried down to the dock by the two older Hawthorne boys. I barely even register Cash, holding up the front end of the vessel. With my eyes hidden behind my sunglasses, I swing my gaze instead to that shirtless, rippling body I've come to know so well already. Luke holds up the back of the kayak, easily bearing the weight with one thick arm. I ogle him unabashedly as he and his brother approach the dock, still amazed that such an ideal man has fallen into my life.

"Jesus Christ," Cash sneers at me and Maddie, "I should have worn some shades down here—that pale ass skin of yours is gonna make me go blind."

"Ha, ha," I say dismissively, "Just wait until you're an old, sunbaked, wrinkly dude at the age of thirty, and then we'll see who's laughing."

"He's already a grumpy old asshole on the inside," Luke says, lowering the kayak from his shoulder, "I'm sure the outside will match before long."

I deliberately refrain from responding to Luke, as per our ground rules. We've gotten pretty good at this whole feigning-indifference thing, I have to say.

"You got the keys to the truck?" Cash asks Luke. I know for a fact that he does. A very large butterfly ricochets around my stomach as I once again recall what, exactly, happened in that truck mere hours ago.

"What do you need it for?" Luke asks, forking over the keys to his brother.

"Need some more smokes," Cash tells him, laughing at Luke's unamused expression, "Sack up, man. It's not meth."

I glance over at the brothers, gaging Luke's reaction. Most of the time, he hides his resentment of his older brother well enough. But when Cash goes and shoves his don't-give-a-fuck bad boy act in Luke's face, it's hard for him to disengage.

"Oh, right. I forgot that lung cancer is real fucking manly," Luke says flatly, "Forget sacking up—when are you gonna try *growing* up, Cash?"

"What would I do that for?" Cash replies, clearly trying to bait Luke into a conflict, "You're already playing man of the house around here, isn't that right little brother?"

"I'm not *playing* at anything, you prick," Luke snarls, "All I'm doing is picking up your slack."

Uneasiness spikes in my blood as I watch Luke's square jaw pulse with anger. Cash has no respect for Luke, no idea of the sacrifices his younger brother had to make after he bailed on the family. All Cash sees in Luke is the son John wishes his oldest had been. And it drives him crazy.

"What a good little boy," Cash sneers, giving Luke a hard punch on the shoulder.

"Don't touch me, asshole," Luke growls at his brother, balling his hands into fists.

"Come on, lil' guy," Cash goes on, shoving Luke across the dock, "You still afraid to take on your big, bad brother?"

I glance over at Maddie as the brothers square off. Luke is just as big and built as his brother—they're evenly matching in strength. But I can never tell how unhinged Cash actually is. I know he's fond of boxing, and MMA, and that uber-macho crap. Luke has too much integrity to resort to violence unless it's absolutely necessary, but Cash...?

"I've always preferred fair fights, Cash. *Clean* fights," Luke tells his brother evenly, "Not exactly your specialty."

Cash's hazel eyes flash with indignant outrage at Luke's words. I have no idea what Luke is alluding to, but whatever it is, it seems to have struck a nerve with his brother.

"Guys, come on. Chill out..." Maddie says, rising to her feet.

"Seriously, you're being idiots," I snap anxiously.

"You girls just aren't used to the way guys settle things," Cash grins.

"The way *some* guys settle things," Luke corrects him sternly, "No matter the consequences. Right, Cash?"

Luke's defiant words only stoke the ire brewing in Cash's eyes. What the hell must have happened to these men to make them so bitter towards each other? What was it that really turned these brothers into nemeses?

"Cash..." Maddie pleads, "Could you please just drop this? You're freaking me out."

"Yeah Luke," I murmur, easing toward him, "This is nuts. You guys are brothers."

"In name, maybe," Luke spits contemptuously, "But thankfully, that's all."

"That's the good ol' Hawthorne name for you," Cash snarls, "It'll stick to you like a motherfucker, even if it doesn't mean shit."

Luke tears his eyes away from his older brother, bitter disappointment showing through his anger.

"Well," Cash goes on haughtily, "I'm off." I feel my body tense up as his hazel eyes dart unexpectedly toward me. "You wanna ride with?"

Luke's head whips around toward his brother, his eyes narrowing suspiciously. I stare back at Cash, taken off guard by his offer. He's barely acknowledged me the entire time we've been here at the house. Why the sudden interest? Still, I can't very well refuse. Part of my strategy for not attracting attention to me and Luke is dividing my time among the other lake house guests. Including Cash, I guess.

"Oh. Uh...OK," I say to Cash, trying to keep the trepidation out of my voice, "Yeah, why not. I haven't really seen much of the town here."

"Great," Cash replies, "Though fair warning, there's not much of a town to see. It's kind of a shit hole, to be honest."

"Well, now I have to see it," I laugh gamely, making sure not to steal a glance at Luke as I grab my things and follow Cash up along the dock. But even though I refrain from looking at my secret companion, I can feel the tense unease rising off of him. He won't stop me from going, but I know he's less than thrilled about it.

"I didn't know those two, uh, got along so well…" I hear Maddie say to Luke as I walk away with Cash.

"Mhm," Luke murmurs in response. I can feel his eyes boring into my back as I walk along in Cash's wake. Is he just angry with his brother after their spat, or is he unhappy with me as well? Is it even safe to be riding along with the unpredictable Cash Hawthorne?

I guess I'm about to find out, one way or another.

"Hop in," Cash says to me as we reach the well-worn family pickup.

I glance back at the truck bed as I yank open the passenger side door. If only this truck could talk, huh? Scrambling up into the seat, I realize that this is the first time I've been alone with Cash since arriving at the lake house. And as he starts the truck, peeling away from the house with one arm dangling out the driver's side window, I wonder if I should have left it that way.

"You guys really don't fuck around, huh?" I laugh nervously, glancing at Luke's glowering face in the rear view mirror as the truck trundles away.

Cash grunts back at me. Not exactly a talker, this one.

"I get the sibling rivalry thing," I try again, tucking my knees into my chest, "Maddie and I can't go fifteen minutes without getting on each other's last—"

"Mind if I put on some music?" Cash cuts me off bluntly, not waiting for my answer before cranking up the radio.

I sink back against my seat, keeping my eyes glued to the road ahead. What the hell did Cash ask me to come along for if he's just going to pretend I'm not here, as usual?

"So you and Luke are school buddies, huh?" Cash shouts over the blaring hard rock.

"Not exactly," I yell back, "We've seen each other around campus is all."

"Really?" Cash challenges me, shooting a devilish grin my way.

"Yeah, really," I snap back, hugging my knees tightly, "What's it to you?"

"The way he's been looking at you lately, I was just wondering," Cash goes on, "I mean, did you see his face when you walked away with me just now?"

I whip around to face the eldest Hawthorne brother. It's only been a few minutes, but I'm well out of patience for this bad boy dickhead routine.

"Is that why you wanted me to come with you? Just to mess with Luke?" I ask pointblank.

"I may have been testing a theory, sure," Cash shrugs.

"And that theory would be...?" I press.

"That my little brother is into you," Cash replies coolly, "And from the way he was acting just now, I'd say that my theory's been proven right."

"Whatever, Cash," I mutter, looking away from him with my heart in my throat.

"What's the matter? Don't you like him back?" Luke's brother toys with me.

"What is this, third grade?" I shoot back at him, "Maybe your little brother is right. You should grow up."

"Ouch," Cash laughs, "You Porter women don't hold any punches, do you?"

"From what I just saw back on the dock, neither do you Hawthorne men," I reply coldly.

"Looks like we're all made for each other, huh?" Cash says quietly, his suddenly pensive eyes hard on the road.

"Guess so," I reply vaguely, wishing that this seat had an ejector button.

Cash ramps up the volume to its highest possible setting, and we drive along the Montana backroads without another word between us.

I decide not to tell Luke about his brother's suspicions straightaway. After their near-brawl, I'm afraid to stoke the tensions between them. I've never seen anything enrage Luke the way Cash manages to. But that's what family is for, right? I don't have to try very hard not to talk about my little jaunt with Cash. When I get back that night, Luke's lips are entirely sealed on the subject. I try and give him some space to cool down, seeking out Anna instead. I want to clear the air after our own spat on the dock. But wouldn't you know it—she's gone off with Finn and his band. Looks like I get a little unexpected "me time" tonight.

The house is empty as I carry a glass of Merlot up to my bedroom and settle down on the window seat overlooking the backyard. I dig my copy of *War and Peace* out of my backpack and let it fall open on my lap, ready to dive back into the epic tale. But try as I might, I can't seem to concentrate. Cash's words from earlier today keep rattling around in my mind.

Looks like we're all made for each other, huh?

I've never been much of a religious person, but I do believe that some things in life are simply out of our hands. Chiefly among those things? Who we happen to fall for. I couldn't have stopped myself from being attracted to Luke, even if I'd tried. But the unknown connection we shared from the start, our parents' romantic history, that was out of our control too. Why should we let the one trump the other? Why should Luke and I be forced to keep our relationship a secret, just because our parents happened to get there first?

And what would happen…if we chose not to keep it a secret after all?

I take a long sip of wine, looking out across the moonlit landscape. A spot of movement catches my eye, down at the end of the dock. The towering figure of John Hawthorne makes my mother look younger than I've ever seen her before. Or maybe, it's the way she's holding herself at his side. She looks relaxed. Happy. At peace. As I watch from my window, John lifts my mother's face to his, laying a kiss on her lips under the rising moon.

My fingers tighten around the stem of the wineglass as I peer down at them. If anyone could understand the feelings I have for Luke, wouldn't it be my mom? She's fallen for a Hawthorne man too, after all. Maybe, just maybe, there could be a way forward for me and Luke that doesn't revolve around deception. I know it's a revolutionary idea, but…what if we just told our parents the truth?

"Well," I laugh to myself, nursing my wine as the moon rises over the still, glassy lake, "I guess there's a first time for everything."

Chapter Nine

It's strange how comfortable this house has come to feel after just one week. By rights, I should want nothing more than to book it back to Sheridan. But against all odds, I've enjoyed my stay here so far. Granted, Luke's presence has been a welcome surprise out here in the middle of nowhere. But there's something wonderful about being removed from the current of daily life, too. Out here, it's like we can all live by our own rules and standards. Who's going to stop us, after all? Maybe that's why my idea of coming clean about my relationship with Luke has started to pick up steam. Our situation may be unconventional, but it's not like there's anyone out here to stop us.

After a long yoga practice on Friday morning, one week after I first arrived here at the lake house, I gather my toiletries and head down the hall for a nice, hot shower. Everyone is scattered around the property, doing their own things, so I don't even have to wait to get into the bathroom—quite the rare occurrence with eight people in the house.

Closing the bathroom door behind me, I shuck off my sweaty yoga clothes and turn on the shower. I perch on the edge of the claw-foot bathtub as the water heats up, letting the warm mist roll over my just-stretched muscles. Rolling my head from side to side, I start to hum softly, wordlessly. It's only been a few weeks since school ended, but I'm already jonesing to perform again. To use my voice and my body, to feel the freedom of giving over to a character, or a piece.

Stepping under the hot spray of the shower, I massage shampoo into my caramel hair, letting my voice swell from deep in my diaphragm. I run through lines of all my favorite songs, moving from folk to rock to soul on a whim. My belting voice echoes off the bathroom tiles as I have at it. My dorm-mate Kim hated it when I sang in the shower—I received *many* a passive-aggressive post-it note about it. But here, in this big empty house, I can really go to town.

A cool draft glances against my wet skin, cutting me off mid-note. I spin around toward the door, mouth clamped shut. Is it possible that the house isn't as empty as I thought?

"Damn," a familiar voice says from the other side of the shower curtain, "Those are some pipes you've got, there."

"Luke!" I squeak, poking my head around the curtain, "What the hell are you doing in here?!"

He's standing with his back against the bathroom door, arms crossed over his chest. His short brown hair is sleep-tousled, and the stubble on his jaw is darker than usual. God, what I wouldn't give for him to be the first thing I saw *every* morning...

"I heard the concert from down the hall. Didn't want to miss it," he grins, taking a swinging stride toward me, "I had no idea you could sing like that, Sophie."

"Yeah, well," I murmur, flattered despite myself, "You still shouldn't be in here."

"Why? I thought bathrooms were sort of our thing?" he goes on, nudging the curtain aside.

My body flushes with want as Luke rakes his eyes along my form. Warm water runs in rivulets around my breasts, down my stomach, over the carefully-kept patch of dark hair between my legs. Someone could walk in any minute and find us here together. But somehow that only makes this sexier.

"Luke," I begin nervously.

"Just let me look at you," he cuts me off, drinking me in with his dark green eyes. "Christ. You're so beautiful."

"You just saying that to get some?" I tease him breathlessly, running my hands through my shower-soaked hair.

"Hardly," Luke grins back, "I don't need to flatter you to get some. I barely even have to touch you before you're all ready for me…"

"You're terrible," I murmur, as Luke runs a hand down my water-slicked arm.

"And you're a dirty little sex fiend," he says, that devilish grin growing wider.

"Did you even bother to lock the door?" I laugh, batting his hand away and turning off the shower, "Or are you *trying* to get us caught?"

"Maybe I am," he shrugs, leaning against the sink as I wrap a towel around my body.

I stop and look up at him in surprise. We may be borderline telepathic at times, but has Luke actually been reading my thoughts word-for-word lately?

"Are you being serious?" I ask him quietly.

"I don't know, Sophie," he says gruffly, shoving a hand through his hair, "I just know that I'm getting sick of hiding. I want to be able to look at you, and talk to you, and touch you whenever I like."

"This wouldn't have anything to do with Cash corralling me along on his errand the other day?" I ask tentatively.

Luke's expression hardens. "Yeah. I wouldn't have minded putting a stop to that shit," he says.

"I'm getting pretty tired of pretending too," I go on carefully, laying a hand on his bicep, "Keeping something like this from Anna, and even from Maddie…it doesn't feel right."

"So…What do you think we should do?" Luke says, turning his body toward mine, "Hire a skywriter or something? Take out a page in the paper?"

"Something a little more subtle would probably do the trick," I smile, "In fact, I don't think we'd even necessarily need to come out and tell everyone, if we wanted to let this secret out."

"No?" he rasps, planting his hands on my hips.

"Nope," I reply, stepping up to him in the steamy air. "All we'd have to do is...stop trying to hide it. Let them figure it out themselves."

"Aren't you worried about how it'll play with them?" Luke asks, leaping into the role of devil's advocate. "I mean, it's a little on the far side of normal, isn't it?"

"Luke, we've been wringing our hands over whether this thing between us is OK for long enough. Who can judge us for having feelings for each other, huh? Who gets to say if this is right or wrong, besides us?"

"I can think of a few people who would have some pretty strong opinions about it," he laughs roughly, pulling me closer, "People, and religious institutions, and courts of law..."

"You know something?" I say softly, laying my hands on his firm chest, "I can't really give two shits about what anyone else thinks. Not anymore."

"You really think the rest of them could handle this being out in the open?" Luke asks me, his green eyes hard on my face.

"Only one way to find out," I reply, hope lifting my voice. I feel like we're standing on a precipice, getting ready to fall or fly.

"Well shit," Luke says, letting out a deep breath, "This just got real."

"That it did," I laugh, circling my arms around his waist. "Just remember, we don't need to make any grand pronouncements. We just have to let it happen, you know? Hell, half our siblings are probably onto us already."

"What do you mean?" Luke asks, cocking an eyebrow.

"I have a feeling that Anna knows something," I confide in him, "And, uh, Cash may also be a little suspicious... He sort of said as much in the truck that day."

"Sonofabitch," Luke mutters, shaking his head with a rueful smile, "So he was just trying to fuck with me, bringing you along?"

"Pretty much," I allow, "See? Everyone will know in no time."

"To be honest, it isn't our brothers and sisters I'm worried about," Luke says, taking a step away from me. "It's my dad. He's never been able to stand it when I step off the straight and narrow. Not for a minute. And this...?"

"Hey," I say firmly, catching his hands in mine, "Just because John and Robin were the first Hawthorne and Porter to fall for each other, doesn't mean they'll be the last. You know as well I do that they'll be over within the month. And then..."

"So you're falling for me, huh Sophie?" Luke asks, his voice rasping low in his register. He's staring at me intently, his eyes doubled in the bathroom mirror as the steam clears away.

"You can't seriously have any question about that," I say softly.

"Maybe not," he replies, giving my hands a firm squeeze, "But I still wouldn't mind hearing you say it."

"Fine," I say, running my thumb against his broad hand, "I think...I'm falling for you, Luke. No, I *know* I am."

He stares at me for a long moment, his gaze boring into mine. It's like he's scoping out the perimeter of my soul, making absolutely sure that no part of me is hidden from him. And despite Danny's warning to keep a little piece of myself tucked away where Luke can't reach it, I let him see all of me. It may be reckless—no, downright insane—but I want to put my whole self in his hands. Even if that means I'll be left in a million pieces should something go wrong between us.

Without a word, Luke raises my hand to his mouth, kissing my palm. His eyes close as he holds me there, caressing his square jaw as he presses his lips to my skin. And then, just as quickly, he breaks away from me, turning toward the door.

"Aren't you gonna say it back?" I ask, clutching my towel close to my chest.

"And ruin the drama, Ms. Acting School? I'd never do that to you," he says, grinning at me over his broad shoulder.

"Ugh. You suck," I laugh, chucking a hand towel at his towering, retreating form.

"You love every minute of it," he replies, cracking open the door to make sure no one's coming. Easing his frame through the doorway, he turns back to me and goes on, "My dad's having me, Cash, and Finn work a job with him today. We'll be gone until late. But...can I take you into town or something tonight? Since we're giving this not-hiding thing a try?"

"What, you mean like...on a date?" I ask, raising an eyebrow.

"Sure," Luke says, "A real live date, if you can believe it."

It hits me that Luke and I have never *been* on an official date before. Not once. And somehow, his asking now feels like a bigger step than any we've taken together so far. And we've taken *quite* a few, by this point.

"Well...OK," I grin, feeling for the world like I'm fourteen years old again, "I'd be happy to go on a date with you, Luke."

"Great," he grins back, closing the door behind him, "I even promise not to beat anyone up this time... Unless they deserve it, of course."

"Of course," I say, rolling my eyes, "Now get out of here. You're letting all the warm air out."

The door closes with a click, and I brace myself against the sink with both hands. It's not just the prospect of a date with Luke that has me all giddy, of course. It's the idea that maybe, just maybe, we won't need to sneak around for that much longer. We might actually have a chance at being a normal couple, here.

Who ever knew that just getting to "normal" could be such a damn miracle?

Chapter Ten

While the boys are away working, Mom decides it's her moment to pounce. The second we Porter women are alone in the lake house, she declares tonight "girl's night", an occasion that none of us has any chance of wiggling out of. *Great*.

"Come on, it'll be fun!" Mom gushes as she herds me out onto the porch. "The four of us haven't had a proper chat in ages. Humor your poor old mother, will you?"

I see that Anna has already been penned in when I step out onto the verandah. She sits before a giant spread of wine, cheese, chocolate, and fruit. Mom definitely pulled out all the stops tonight, that's for sure. But while I certainly don't ever mind the sight of a few good bottles of red, I can hear that old alarm bell winding up in the back of my mind. Why the special treatment all of a sudden?

"Now let me just get your sister, and we'll be all set," Mom beams, twirling away in a cloud of golden curls and flowing layers.

Anna and I sit quietly on the porch, the night sounds of insects and other creatures rising up around us like a symphony. We still haven't had a second to talk since the other day on the dock. In all honesty, I don't even know where she's been, for the last couple of days.

"You want first dibs?" I offer, nodding at the impressive spread.

"Yeah. Sure," she says disinterestedly, plucking a single strawberry from the fruit plate and popping it into her mouth. I reach for the wine key and set to work uncorking a bottle of Malbec. I know what my priorities are.

"What have you been up to, these past few days?" I ask her point blank, pouring two generous glasses of wine. "I haven't seen hide or hair of you."

"I told you," she says flatly, "I've been hanging out with Finn and his band. Taking some pictures for them."

"For *days*?" I press

"It's not like there's anyone to hang out with here," she replies, flicking her eyes over to me, "What with you and Maddie making yourselves scarce, and all."

There it is. The same accusatory tone my little sister leveled at me the other day by the water. I don't mind confrontation with her or anyone. But I have my suspicions about why she's angry. And if I let her air her grievances, she may very well make me account for my history with Luke. Not to mention my present with him. The two of us have been trying to avoid this very thing from happening since we got here. But now, after our conversation this morning, everything has changed. I can stop lying to my sister. All I have to do is let her ask her questions. The rest will take care of itself…I hope.

"Anna," I begin, taking a deep steadying breath, "I'm sorry."

"For what?" she asks, peering at me over the rim of her wineglass.

"For making you feel like I don't trust you," I go on, lowering my gaze, "For not checking in with you to make sure you were OK."

"Are we talking about *now*, or these whole past few years?" she asks coolly.

"Both? I guess?" I tell her, floundering. "I just want you to know that I do trust you. More than anyone in the world. I want you to be a bigger part of my life, Anna. And I'm sorry if I haven't let you be before. If there's…If there's anything I can do. If there's anything you want to know, or ask me…Well, I'm all ears. And no lip, for once in my damn life."

"Really?" she asks, eyebrows raised.

"Really," I assure her, leaning forward in my Adirondack chair. "Go on, Anna. Ask me."

My little sister chews on her lip, looking away from me as she weighs her next words carefully. I can see her mulling over the options, wondering whether or not she even wants the truth from me now. But when she next looks up at me, I know she's made her choice. This is it. The moment of truth.

"Sophie," she begins quietly, "Are you—?"

"Got her!" Mom's singsong voice bursts from the doorway, making Anna and I jump out of our skins, "Maddie will be down in just a second."

I fall back against my chair, frustrated and disappointed. We were *so* close. I can sense Anna's dismay as well, and lift my blue eyes to her matching ones.

We'll talk soon, I try to assure her with my eyes alone.

And if I had to guess, I'd say that her look translates to, *You bet your ass we will.*

Maddie finally graces us with her presence, stepping out to take the last seat at our impromptu feast. I watch the same pang of suspicion shoot through her body as she takes in the spread. Mom only goes above and beyond like this when something is wrong.

I sit up like a shot as a sudden, beautiful thought occurs to me. What if she's gathered us all out here to let us know that she and John are finally breaking up? What if this is our last night at the lake house, and John's giving her some space to break the news while he gets the boys up to speed? To Mom and John, parting ways might seem like another disappointment for their kids. If only they knew what a blessing such a parting would be. Buoyed by my theory, I settle back in my seat, happily nursing my

wine. I even go so far as to humor my mom's small talk—
that's how good of a mood I'm in.

"I think it's very smart of you, getting some extra
credits over the summer," my Mom says, as the
conversation babbles happily along.

"I just want the option of graduating early, if anything
good comes up," I tell her, "Acting apprenticeships are
pretty competitive. If I snag a good one in the middle of
senior year, I want to be able to grab it."

"Campus must be pretty quiet in the summer," Mom
continues, heaping a plate with cheese and crackers, "I'm
sure it'll be relaxing to get some alone time."

"Not that you'll be entirely without company," Anna
speaks up pointedly. I glance over at her quickly. Does she
know that Luke is going to working on campus this
summer?

"Oh! Will some of your friends be doing the summer
session too?" Mom chirps, "How fun."

"Uh. Kind of," I mutter. May as well give this truth-
telling thing a shot. "It, uh, turns out that Luke is going to
be TA-ing some more classes this session…And he's
going to be an RA, too."

"RA? What's that?" Mom asks me.

"A resident assistant," I clarify, "It means he'll be
living in the dorms, too. Making sure us kiddos don't get
into any trouble."

"Get out," Mom gasps, grabbing for my hand, "That
is so, so wonderful. And here I thought all you kids were
going to go your separate ways after this week. I'm so glad
you two will get to keep on being friends."

"Uh-huh," I reply, trying to keep my cool.

Holy crap…I was right. With all this talk about
"going our separate ways" and "staying friends", Mom
must be working up to telling us that she and John are
splitsville! I can't believe how good this timing is. Just
when Luke and I are getting ready to come clean about our

status, it turns out there's nothing dirty about what we're doing. Not anymore.

"I guess Sophie and Luke will have to be the ones keeping in touch for us all us, huh?" Anna says, dragging my attention back to the conversation, "Since the rest of us will be going home after this?"

"Seems that way," Maddie adds, her voice a bit stilted.

I look around at my mom and sisters, excitement flooding me from head to toe. It will be such a relief to tell them about how I really feel for Luke. Sure, it might be a little awkward for Mom down the line, Luke being her ex's—or rather, double-ex's—son and all. But I'm sure she'll be onto the next guy by then, anyway.

"Well, actually…" my Mom says, a small smile creeping across her face, "I wanted to talk to you girls about just that."

Oh my god. This is it. The moment that will change everything for me and Luke.

"What's up, Mom?" I ask, trying to keep the excitement out of my voice.

"Well," Mom sighs, sipping her wine with no small bit of drama, "I know I told you that my plan for this summer was to spend a little time getting grounded in my hometown before going back to Vermont. Really, I just wanted a couple of weeks away from it all. At first."

I watch my sisters' faces become uneasy, and feel my own expression reflecting theirs'. I wish she would just spit out the good news already, before I have a conniption.

"Are you staying for longer, then?" Anna asks her, brow furrowed, "Did you find another place to rent in town or something?"

"Or something," Mom bubbles, smile widening. She has that mischievous glint in her eye that almost always spells trouble. A cold spike of dread pierces my gut as she goes on. Have I completely misjudged this situation? And if so, what fresh hell is she about to spring on us?

"Actually…" Mom trills, glancing around at us conspiratorially, "God, I feel like a teenager again, dishing with you girls like this. But actually, things have been going so well for me and John here that he's…he's invited me to stay!"

I feel the wind rush out my lungs as my body goes stone still. The alarm that was only a whisper moments ago raises its voice to a keening wail. And all it keeps saying is, "NO. NO. *NO.*"

"You mean like, for another couple of weeks…?" Maddie asks quickly.

"And another, and another," Mom beams, oblivious to the distress on her daughters' faces. As fucking usual.

"Mom, just cut to the chase, OK?" I snap at her, my heart dashing itself against my ribcage, "Exactly how long are you going to stay here playing house with John?"

"Watch your tone," Mom shoots back at me, her airy demeanor suddenly run through with fire, "But since you ask, I'm planning on staying indefinitely."

There it is. The nail in the coffin. Not only can Luke and I not come forward about our feelings now, I'm not sure we can even be a "we" anymore. If Mom and John are taking the next step in their relationship, if this isn't just a fling after all but a full-fledged relationship…there's no way Luke and I can keep pretending that what we're doing isn't wrong.

For the first time since meeting Luke, acidic shame starts to eat away at me. This incredible, life-changing thing we found in each other has, in a moment, become something sick. Something we should be embarrassed about. Something we should bury deep inside ourselves and never drag out into the light of day again.

And I'm not sure I'll ever be able to forgive my mother for that.

"But…You don't live here," Anna sputters, sounding far younger than her years, "You live in Vermont. In our house. The house we've always lived in."

"Yes, dear," Mom snaps impatiently, "I know. I have been living in that house much longer than any of you. And since you're planning to move out to go 'find yourself', Anna, I'd soon be living there all alone. Or I would have been, if John hadn't offered—"

"Are you… Selling our house?" Maddie cuts her off.

"I am planning to sell the house, yes," Mom replies without ceremony.

"But that's—you can't—were you even going to talk to us about it?!" I shout, feeling the world fall away beneath my feet.

"That's what I'm doing now," Mom sighs, exasperated, "Not that I need your permission, but I'm taking my time weighing the decision to—"

"Really? Because it seems to me like you've already made your choice," I cut in, "We love that house, Mom. Our whole childhoods, our entire lives with Dad was there. That place is all we have left of him. We can't lose—"

"Don't tell me about loss," Mom spits back at me, her entire demeanor transforming. All week, we've only been seeing her bright and cheery side. But now that dark streak of hers has come out to play. "I know all about loss, thank you. Your father was the love of my life, from the time I was just a girl. You'll never be able to feel the loss of him the way I have."

"Christ, Mom…" Maddie says disgustedly, "Are you seriously making our grief into a pissing contest right now?"

"Of course not," Mom replies sharply, "Because it's no contest whatsoever. Your father is a part of your past. You can all move on and lead long, happy lives now. But he was my future. My entire future. I've lost more than you can possibly imagine, losing him."

Maddie falls back against the chair, shocked by our mother's unfeeling, deluded response. But honestly? I wish I was surprised by her callousness. By now, her disregard for us isn't shocking. It's just disappointing as hell.

"What would you even know about what we've all been going through since Dad died?" Maddie says softly, "In the past three years, you haven't bothered to check in with any of us about how we were doing. Not once. You don't know the first thing about how his death has changed our lives."

"Please," Mom says, waving her hand dismissively, "I think I know my own daughters—"

"Did you know I've been seriously depressed for the last three years?" Maddie cries, "Did you know that I barely made it through the first semester back at school after he died? That I almost dropped out just before graduating? I talked about being a literature professor like him for my entire life. Did you ever wonder why I suddenly changed my mind and punted to marketing? It's because reading the books he loved, following in his footsteps, was too painful for me once he was gone. His death has changed my entire life. My entire future. Not a day goes by that I don't think of him. And all that's to say nothing of your other two daughters."

I stare up at my big sister, my heart wringing painfully in my chest. I've never heard Maddie speak so bluntly about her own struggles with Dad's death. While I was off working through my own grief, she was all alone on the West Coast with no one to help her through hers. Mom's body goes rigid as she throws her gaze my and Anna's way.

"Is this how you girls feel as well?" she asks us, "That I've been 'negligent to your needs' since Archie passed away? Hmm?"

Anna's blue eyes harden to stone as they fix on Mom's face. "I don't know if you can say 'negligent.' Since you never considered our needs in the first place. I'd say indifferent, if anything."

I stare at my little sister, taken aback. She never calls Mom out on her shit, preferring to protect her feelings and let her keep on living in the fantasy world she's created. Christ, do I know anything about my sisters at all?

"That's ridiculous!" Mom says heatedly.

"Why bother asking if you're just going to shoot us down?" Anna shouts back, "The truth is, Mom, that we've been taking care of you since Dad died."

"Especially Anna," I say, finally picking my jaw up off the floor, "I got to run off to drama school and deal with shit on my own, but she was left to pick up the pieces while you collapsed. We know that Dad's passing was hard on you. Of course it was. But how can you say that we didn't feel it too? How can you know so little about your own kids and not even care?"

"Well," Mom says, rising to her feet, "If this is the way you feel, then I'd think you'd be happy to be rid of me. I'll stay here with John, and take myself off your hands for good."

"For good?" I cry, pulling all the punches now, "Mom, be serious. You've had plenty of flings since dad died. How is this one any different? You're putting our family, our home, everything at stake for him. Please, just take a second to consider—"

"You've given me plenty to consider tonight," Mom interrupts me, "I've apparently failed you as a mother, isn't that right? You'd be better off without me?"

"That's not what we're saying at all, Mom," Maddie whispers, "What I've wanted more than anything else since dad died was my mother. I've always wanted you to be a part of my life. Please don't make that impossible."

"I see," Mom replies with disdain, "Well, girls. Thank you for making this decision so easy for me. Since I'm apparently incapable of being a good mother to you, I'll just go ahead and bow out. Seeing as I'm impossible. Anna, you're more than welcome to stay at the Vermont house until it's sold. Though I suggest finding other accommodations quickly. I'm sure that property will get snatched up quick."

With that, she turns away and leaves us there on the porch. Here one moment, gone the next. Same as ever. Only this time, she has no idea of the heartache she leaves in her wake. The world goes blurry around me as tears flood my vision, coursing hotly down my cheeks.

"I just... I can't believe her," I mutter.

"I can," Anna spits, "As far as I'm concerned, this is pretty in-character for good ol' Robin."

"Do you think she'll really stay here with John?" Maddie asks us both plaintively, "Maybe she's just bluffing."

"Now she'll stay, just to spite us," I say bitterly. "Where do you think you got your competitive streak from, Maddie? We've dared to challenge her. Now we're the ones who are going to pay."

A sudden thought occurs to me in my desperate despair, and I put words to it before I can think.

"Fuck her," I snap, "If she cares that little about us, why don't we just follow her lead? What if we just took a stand and cut her out of our lives, right now? If the three of us broke off from her, think of how much happier—"

"If any of us could stand to abandon her completely, we would have already," Maddie cuts in, "No matter how badly she hurts us, she's still family. That's not something you can ever forget."

My heart sinks as I realize that she's right. Family isn't something you can wash away, no matter how many tears you shed over the ways it disappoints you. I almost have to laugh at the irony of it all. Your family is supposed to be made up of the people who care about you the most. But now, I'm being kept from the person I care about most, *because* of my family.

Not exactly "ha ha" funny, is it?

My ears prick up at the sound of a car engine approaching the lake house. The men must be back from their job. I look up toward the driveway and spot the family pickup lumbering our way. Cash drives while John rides shotgun, the truck loaded down with wooden planks and slabs of concrete. And there, sitting in the truck bed with his little brother, is Luke.

The sight of him sends a punishing blow of despair straight into my solar plexus. Suddenly, there's no denying the reality of my mom's decision to stay here with John. No getting around this obstacle that's sprung up in my path. I know that I should stay here, tell Luke the news myself…but I can't bear to watch the happiness go out of his eyes when he realizes that we're through.

Hating myself for it, I turn away from him. I dash away through the front door at the same moment that Anna runs off down the front stairs. My bare feet carry me through the cavernous house, out through the patio door, and down toward the lake's edge. I sprint out onto the dock, tears blurring my vision. After just a few furious paces, I feel my feet fly out from under me as I hit a slick patch on the wooden planks. I pitch forward, my hands shooting out in front of me to break my fall.

Sharp pain shoots up through my arms as I land hard, my wrists taking the full force of my impact with the dock. Rolling onto my back, I hiss out my pain through gritted teeth as the clear night sky careens overhead. Only now, as I lay here leveled, do I let the full weight of my despair roll over me. Deep, wrenching sobs rip out of my throat, carrying out across the still water of the lake. Laying here, alone between the water and the sky, I feel smaller than I ever have in my life. Just when I thought the universe was on my side, I find myself out of its good graces once more.

My voice catches in my throat as the sharp sound of screaming shatters the night air. I pull myself to sitting on the slippery dock, cradling my aching left wrist to my chest. Raised male voices ring out from the front of the house. At first, it's only John and Cash that are yelling out there like madmen. But then I hear Luke's voice as well, raised in outrage. I've never heard him like this, before. Not even that night at The Bear Trap, when he stopped me and Danny from getting attacked. The ire comes through loud and clear in Luke's every shouted syllable, but there's something deeper rumbling beneath his anger.

It's pain.

The shouting voices give way to sounds of fierce struggle, and icy panic floods my body. Luke's told me about how his father used to hit him and his brothers when they were small. I had no idea that threat of violence still existed. I would expect a man who hits children to be too cowardly to fight with anyone his own size. But as the men's screaming reaches a fever pitch, there can be no doubt of what's unfolding out there in the dark.

Before I can form a single rational thought, I scramble to my feet and start sprinting for the house. My wrist throbs painfully with every step I take, but I couldn't stop now if I tried. The hurt in his voice matches my own pain. Our sorrow is vibrating on the same frequency, and his draws me to him now. I fly across the grassy lawn, no plan in mind to stop the men from beating each other into the ground…

But it looks like I won't need one.

I skid to a stop as Luke storms around the side of the house. He's unhurt, as far as I can see. And thank god for that. His shoulders are drawn up, his hands balled into furious fists. His strong, square jaw is set like concrete, and his mouth in a straight, grave line. But it's his eyes that do me in—his pained, furious, perfect green eyes. The same eyes that have seen to the very core of me, in whose gaze I've found deeper understanding than I could have ever hoped possible, are alight with anguish. And the second they land on me, a fresh wave of tears washes over me.

Luke catches me up in his arms as I run to him, burying my face in his chest as I weep. He holds me tightly to him, bracing me as I shake with sobs. We don't need to ask the other what's happened, the shared source of our despair is perfectly clear. Our parents have decided to advance their relationship, which means a future between me and Luke is impossible. Even the rest of the summer, which we were supposed to spend together at Sheridan, has been ripped away from us.

"It's not fair," I whisper fiercely, looking up at Luke.

"No," he growls, wiping the tears from my face with his thumbs, "No it's fucking not."

"What are we going to do?" I breathe, clutching my throbbing wrist, "Luke—"

"What happened?" he demands, gently taking hold of my left arm.

"It's stupid," I mutter, shaking my head, "I was upset, and I lost my footing—"

"It's swollen," he says through gritted teeth, "Probably sprained."

"Don't worry about me," I say, "What about you? Are you OK? I heard—"

"We need to set this," he cuts me off, leading me back around the house to the garage. "I'm sure I have a splint from one of my sports injuries upstairs."

He won't let me ask about the fight, that much is clear. Dazed, I give in and follow him to the garage. His car is parked there, and I steady myself against the trunk as we reach it.

"Wait here," Luke tells me, planting a kiss on the top of my head, "I'll be right back."

I nod silently, and Luke disappears into the house. For a moment, all is silent again. But just as I start to take a breath, I hear the shriek of tires peeling out of the driveway. Rushing forward, I catch a glimpse of the family pickup charging away at top speed. And standing there, watching it go, is my sister. Maddie. Her body is rooted to the ground, still as stone. She looks as gutted as I feel. I take a step toward her, hoping to offer what comfort I can, but she turns and bolts into the house just as Luke reappears in the garage doorway.

"Here," he says, holding up a small sling, "I must have been fourteen when I needed this, so it should fit you fine."

"Ha, ha," I smile tremblingly, as Luke helps me work my arm into the brace, "Good to know your sense of humor is still intact. I have a feeling we'll be needing it."

But he doesn't respond as he ministers to my injury. Each minute of silence that unfolds between us feels like another brick in the wall that's rising up to separate us. Just as I muster up the courage to speak, the sound of a slamming car door jerks my attention away. I turn to see Maddie hoisting her heavy suitcase into her secondhand car and hurrying into the driver's seat. She takes off like a shot down the driveway. And I know for certain that she's not coming back.

"This whole thing is falling to pieces," I breathe.

"That's for damn sure," Luke replies, helping me to standing. Once he sees that I'm stable, he goes back to the garage door and grabs something else from inside.

It's my suitcase. And another that must be his.

"What are you doing with those?" I ask softly.

"We're leaving, Sophie," he tells me, "I'm getting you out of here."

"We can't just leave...Can we?" I breathe, as Luke walks around me and heaves our bags into the trunk of his car. "Nothing's been solved, here."

"And nothing ever will be," Luke says heatedly, slamming the trunk, "What just happened with my dad? That's not news, Sophie. That's been my entire life. And now this thing with your mom? And what it means for us...? Fuck it. I'm done."

"Maybe we should just think this over. For a second," I offer quietly.

"Look at your arm, Sophie," Luke growls back, "You got hurt, because of this. Because of *them*. I don't trust my dad enough to keep you in this house with him. We're going back to Sheridan tonight. It's safer there, believe me."

Cold fear runs down my spine as I see that Luke is truly afraid of what his father is capable of. What must this man have done to his sons to warrant such fear?

"Look. Maddie's already gone," Luke says firmly, "I'm sure Anna will be right on her heels. Just please, say you'll come with me now, Sophie."

"I...I'm not sure..." I stall, shaking my head.

"Well I am," he says shortly, "Trust me to take the lead on this."

"I do trust you, Luke," I say softly.

"Then prove it," he growls, "And get in the damn car."

Numb and exhausted, I follow his orders and clamber clumsily into the passenger's seat. My final view of the lake house dissolves into a kaleidoscopic blur as tears rush in to obscure my vision. How such a beautiful place has played host to such chaos, I'll never understand. But if there's one thing I do understand, it's the rush of relief I feel the second Luke and I hit the open road. As long as we're in this together, there's still a thread of hope to hang onto.

Though I can't say I wouldn't prefer something a little stronger than a thread.

Chapter Eleven

Just a couple hours later, shortly before midnight, Luke turns onto the darkened Sheridan campus. The place is absolutely deserted on this summer night. And while I should be comforted by the sight of these familiar lawns and halls, the eerie, dead quiet of the empty campus ruins the effect.

It's a week earlier than I was meant to return to school for summer classes. Luckily, I got to keep my dorm room from spring semester, so I still have the key. At least there's a place for me to rest my head, in the midst of all the chaos that's erupted tonight. And at least I get to share that place with Luke for the time being.

He's been nearly silent for the entire drive. I can't even begin to guess at the contents of his mind. Luke's had to be the responsible, loyal son among the Hawthorne boys his entire life. For him to have left with me tonight is a huge departure from that role. I don't blame him for not wanting to talk about it right away. When he's ready, he'll tell me his thoughts. I hope.

We roll to a stop in front of my dorm. Not a single light is on in the entire hall. I glance over at Luke, sitting motionless in the driver's seat.

"Did we just ditch a family drama for a horror movie?" I joke softly, "This place looks creepy as hell, all empty."

"It's still better than being back at that house," Luke says, cutting the engine and swinging himself out of the car.

I push open the passenger side door and step out into the night. Luke falls back into silence as he grabs my suitcase out of the trunk, leaving his for a second trip since I can't exactly carry anything. He walks past me to the front door of the dorm, unlocking it with his Sheridan ID card.

"You know this dorm?" I ask him, stepping into the building in his wake.

"Yep," Luke replies, nodding at the security guard, "I used to live here, too."

"Small world," I say quietly, as he summons the elevator. But he doesn't reply as we step inside. My pulse quickens anxiously. Something feels off, here…between us. He's stonewalling me in a way he hasn't done since I was his smitten student. And I don't like it one bit.

The elevator doors whisper open, and we walk down the hall toward my room. Our footsteps echo loudly on the tile, the only sound save for the humming of the fluorescent bulbs overhead. I catch a glimpse of myself in a darkened study room window. The harsh light casts dark shadows under my tear-swollen eyes. My long hair is pulled into a hasty top knot, and the sling glares ominously against my white tank top. I look like a complete mess. But that stands to reason, since I feel like one too.

"Here we are," I say, my voice artificially light as I unlock my dorm room and step inside. I take a deep breath, savoring the familiar scents of sage incense and dark coffee. Already, the lake house is starting to feel like part of another dimension. Some place far removed from my real life—the real life where Luke isn't my almost-brother, but a sexy teacher with a nose for justice. Being back here, I almost believe that we can put the events of this last week behind us.

…Almost.

"Do you have everything you need?" Luke asks, setting down my bag, "Ice packs for your wrist, Advil, all that?"

"I'm a dancer, remember?" I remind him, "I've got ice packs and Advil for days."

"Good," he says, shoving his hands deep into his pockets, "That's...good."

We stare at each other across the living room, unspeaking. There's only a few feet of space between us, but I've never felt farther away from him. His face is entirely unreadable, that easy understanding we've come to share is totally out of my reach. A sense of foreboding hangs over me like a swollen cloud, ready to burst. But maybe if I don't glance up, it'll disperse on its own.

"You up for a movie or something?" I ask him, turning into the kitchen, "I don't think I can sleep just yet. I've got some snacks left over here, too. Do you like popcorn? That's a stupid question. Who doesn't like popcorn?"

"Sophie..." Luke says from the doorway, his voice harsh. He hasn't taken a step into my room.

"Maybe we can push the two beds together for tonight?" I go on, purposely not hearing him, "Something tells me you're not gonna fit in a twin with me. Oh! Or we could just lay out all the couch cushions and—"

"Sophie, stop," Luke rasps. I force myself to take a deep breath and look back at him from the kitchen. He's standing there in front of the door, his feet rooted in the ground. Pain and frustration grip his sculpted features.

"What is it?" I ask quietly, not wanting to hear the answer.

"I just wanted to make sure you got back here safely," Luke says, his jaw set, "But I can't stay here. You know that."

"Oh..." I reply, my voice straining through my throat, "That's right. You've got your own room on campus, right? Since you're going to be an RA? That's cool, if you want to sleep there—"

"No," Luke growls, his hands clenching into fists, "It's not about the room, Sophie. It's about... Everything else. I can't be here. At Sheridan. Not now."

"Wh-what do you mean?" I stammer, "That was the plan. We were going to come back here together and have the rest of our summer."

"You know that's impossible now," Luke says firmly, fixing his green eyes on me. "I can't stay here with you, Sophie."

"But...I don't understand..." I breathe, steadying myself against the kitchen doorway, "You *have* to stay. You're teaching, aren't you?"

"I'll let the school know that something's come up," he says shortly, "I'm done with this place. For good."

"And me?" I ask tremulously, "Are you done with me, too?"

Luke looks at me in silence, and I watch as his green eyes harden into stone. He's pulling away from me. Drawing up his defenses. Getting ready to lock me out forever.

"Luke," I say quickly, moving toward him across the room, "I know that tonight has been hard. With everything going on with our parents, and—"

"Hard doesn't begin to cover it, Sophie," he cuts me off, shaking his head.

"That's fair," I say, keeping my distance, "But isn't that all the more reason we should try and get through it together? I mean—"

"Wake up, Sophie," Luke roars suddenly, striking the wooden door with his fist, "We *can't* be together. Not anymore."

"Luke, calm down," I tell him, backing away from his towering form. He catches sight of me shrinking back and shoves a hand roughly through his short brown hair.

"Look at me, would you?" he growls through gritted teeth, "Now I've scared you. Jesus Christ... I'm just like him."

"Who...Your dad?" I breathe, stopping dead in my tracks, "You're nothing like him, Luke."

"Then how did I get saddled with his fucking life?" Luke demands furiously, blinded by resentment and rage. I've never seen him like this, on the edge of losing control. And I can't lie, it *does* scare me.

"If you'd just talk to me, Luke, maybe we could figure something out," I venture.

"There's nothing to talk about," he says harshly, "You know as well as I do that this thing is impossible now. They've ruined it for us. It's over."

"It doesn't have to be," I whisper, willing myself not to cry, "We don't have to give them the final say, Luke."

"No," he says with grave finality, "We don't have to give it to them. They've had it all along. I'm sorry. I need to get out of here."

"Look, I don't need to be here for summer classes," I cut in, "Let me come with you. We can just go off together, start all over."

"Don't be crazy," he shoots me down, "You need to be here, doing what you love. Getting your future all squared away."

Because I won't be a part of it. That's what he's really trying to tell me. That I need to get on with my life without him, and I might as well start now. God knows, he's going to.

"Please don't do this Luke," I plead softly, balling my trembling hands into tight fists, "Please don't leave me here."

"I know it's hard. But one day, you'll thank me for not dragging this thing out," he says, not looking at me.

"This thing?" I laugh bitterly, "Is that what you'd call us? Just some *thing*?"

"I'm going to go now," he says, turning away from me, "Before you say something you'll regret in the morning."

"The only thing I regret is trusting you to be different," I snap at him, "Trusting you not to hurt me like everyone else has."

"Don't turn this into some kind of melodrama," he says meanly, looking at me over his shoulder, "We're not in acting class, Soph."

"Fuck you," I whisper, "Get out of my room."

Without a word of response, he does just that, striding out of my dorm room with his shoulders squared. I rush across the space and slam the door shut behind him, snapping the lock into place with a decisive click. I listen to his retreating footsteps, barely audible over the sound of my pounding heart. Only once I've heard the elevator doors open and shut do I let that dark cloud of despair break over me.

Pressing my back to the wooden door, I slide down onto the ground. I pull my knees tightly to my chest, letting the tears come hard and fast. I don't make a sound as sorrow swells up all around me. I don't cry and sob to the unfeeling heavens, like I did back on the dock. I'm speechless, voiceless in the face of this incredible, inevitable pain.

You brought this on yourself, you know, some malicious little part of me says over and over again in the silence of my empty room, *You brought this on yourself.*

And it's true. I asked for this. I've been courting this heartache since that first day at the lake house, when I discovered the truth about Luke's family and mine. I could have cut ties with him right then and there, saved myself from this unbelievable hurt. Maybe Luke is right about me. Maybe I'm more interested in being the star of my own little melodrama than I am in the people I care about most. Maybe I'm just a pathetic, masochistic little drama queen who's had it coming all along.

Well...What better company for a drama queen than her drama king?

In a daze, I dig my cell phone out of my backpack and type out a message with trembling fingers.

Me: Are you near campus? I need you.

By the time I've managed to pour myself onto the well-worn couch, I've received my reply.

Danny: I'm near-ish. What's going on? Is this a booty call? I thought Sexy Pants was taking care of all your needs these days.

Me: I'm afraid Sexy Pants has flown the coop. Everything's gone to shit, Danny.

Danny: Where are you?

Me: In my dorm. He just left.

A long moment passes while Danny takes in my message. But finally, he replies.

Danny: I'm coming. Just stay put.

Me: Thank you, Danny.

Danny: That's what boy friends are for, right? For when actual boyfriends fuck up.

A sound that's part laugh, part sop rips out of my throat at Danny's message. I curl up on the couch, waiting for my best friend to arrive. He may not be able to understand how I've let myself fall so hard, but I know he'll offer me a hand as I right myself again…and a swift kick in the ass if I let myself mope too long.

The perfect combination for a broken-hearted mess like me.

***

The one precious week I got to spend at the lake house with Luke flew by in one sweeping rush. The following week, however, moves so slowly that I find myself wondering if time has simply stopped. With no classes, no work, no tasks to distract me, the ache of Luke's absence is amplified tenfold. Danny does his best to keep me company, but I can tell that even his patience with my despondency is wearing thin. By the time the week has come and gone, he's had it with my lovesickness.

"If you're not gonna eat that burrito, I am," he snaps at me across the table. We've hunkered down at Pequeño for a little pre-summer semester feast. Classes start up again tomorrow, and by rights I should be thrilled. But mustering up even an ounce of enthusiasm is proving to be impossible.

"Have at," I say to Danny, pushing my plate across the table, "I'm not hungry."

"You've barely eaten anything all week," he says, crossing his arms, "You wanna pass out on our first day of classes and embarrass yourself in front of everyone? You know we have guest artists coming in from New York City to teach us, right? Artists who have theater companies, and connections, and zero tolerance for mopey bullshit."

"Are you trying to make me feel worse about all this?" I ask him, taking a long swig of my margarita, "I haven't heard a word from Luke since he ditched me here last week. I don't know where he is, or what he's doing.

My sisters and I haven't even had a chance to get on the same page about what to do with our mother—"

"Babe," Danny cuts me off, reaching across the table and taking my hands, "You've got a whole lot to say about Luke, and Anna, and Maddie. But you know who you should really be worried about right now? *Sophie*."

"Wh-what?" I stammer, "What do you mean?"

"You have no way of controlling what Luke does next," Danny says, brushing his thumb against my hand, "He's going to make his own choices, and he'll have to live with them. The only thing you have control over is what *you* do now. You can choose to self-destruct and waste this summer feeling sorry for yourself. Or you can choose to pull yourself the fuck together, kill it for those New York people, and keep on chasing the dreams you had long before Luke Hawthorne stuck it to you. So, what's it gonna be Sophie? What's your move?"

I stare at Danny for a long, hard moment as his words hit home. With slow deliberation, I take my hands from his, reach across the table, and pull my plate back toward me. A smile blooms across my face as I pick up my gigantic, glorious burrito and take a monster-sized bite out of it.

"That's my girl," Danny crows, thumping his fist on the table, "Sophie Porter rides again!"

"You'd better believe it, buddy," I reply, tucking into my meal.

Deep down, I know that this new I-don't-give-a-fuck attitude is an act. My bruised heart still aches for Luke with every single beat. But maybe if I really commit to pretending like I'm OK, I'll actually start to feel a little better. Maybe a little "method acting" is exactly what's called for, here. That and another order of tortilla chips, that is.

A couple hours later, I arrive back at my dorm room with a full belly, a nice buzz, and a newfound determination to make the most of this summer. With or, more likely, without Luke Hawthorne to share it. I flop down on my bed and go to set an early alarm on my cell phone—I want to have enough time in the morning for a nice long run before the first day of summer classes.

Unbidden, the memory of racing through the woods with Luke as my guide rises in my mind's eye. I see his tanned, broad shoulders moving rhythmically as his strong, balanced figure leads me forward. I see his wide grin, his sharp scruffy jaw, that sweep of chestnut hair backlit by the breaking day as we reach the summit. And of course, I see him lowering that perfect body to mine, feel the enormity of him parting me, filling me, making me whole...

"No," I mutter to myself in the dark, empty dorm room, "You can cut that shit out, right now."

Maybe just pretending like I'm over Luke isn't going to be enough, here. Maybe I need to actually do something about it. It's been a week since I've seen him, and I've had no word from him at all. I haven't made any contact either, but I'm not the one who bailed. The ball has been in his court to open the lines of communication. But you know what? I think it's about time I took that ball and headed on home.

I set my jaw and open up a new message on my phone, entering Luke's number. Without taking a spare moment to think, lest I lose my nerve, I write:

Me: Hey Luke. Just wanted to let you know that everything is good here. My wrist is even healed. Thank you for all your help, and for getting me back here safely. I was upset to see you go, but I understand that it's for the best. You're right—carrying on any further is just asking for trouble. I won't come chasing after you or anything crazy

```
like that, I just want you to know that
I loved getting to know and spend time
with you, however short that time
seemed. Take care of yourself.
```

I let my phone fall onto the bed as I roll onto my side, hugging my knees to my chest. Where will Luke even be when he gets my message? Back at the lake house? Out on the road? Across the country? I haven't the slightest idea. My head jerks up as I hear my phone ping softly, and see Luke's name attached to a new text. I snatch up the phone, holding my breath as I take in his response.

```
Luke: Good to know. Have a good
summer.
```

A rasping laugh escapes my throat as I read his text. Have a good summer? That's the sort of thing an acquaintance would write in someone's high school year book—and a passing acquaintance at that. He's treating me just like he used to, back when he was nothing more than my sexy TA—with cool nonchalance. Amiable disinterest. Well, fine. Like Danny said, there's nothing I can do to control his actions from here on out. If he's going to treat me like a stranger, I just have to accept it.

…But that still doesn't keep the silent tears from streaming down my face as I sink into a numb, dreamless sleep.

Chapter Twelve

Against all odds, I find myself settling into a new routine as summer classes commence. For nine hours a day, I attended workshops and one-on-one training sessions with an incredible group of teachers, including my beloved (if occasionally prickly) movement instructor, Gary, who's running the show. There are only eight of us students who were selected to take part in these rigorous classes, and by the end of each day I'm too exhausted to dwell on my stalled love life, the impending sale of my childhood home, or anything else that's going on beyond the walls of Sheridan. Sure, I'll have to deal with all of those things someday. But for the next couple of weeks, I at least get to set my baggage down for a spell.

At the end of the first two weeks of summer classes, all eight of us students are supposed to have a private meeting with Gary to discuss our progress so far. I head over to his office in the performing arts building at the end of the day on Friday, excited to talk about what I'm learning as a performer in this intensive atmosphere. Gary's alone in his office when I arrive, his balding head bent over his desk. I rap my knuckles on the open door.

"Hey Gare," I smile brightly, "How's tricks?"

"Oh. Sophie. Good," he says, having none of my sunny disposition, "Come on in and close the door, would you?"

I do as he says, slightly put off by his less-than-enthusiastic tone. My teacher's eyes follow me as I cross the room and settle into a chair before him. I thought these were going to be informal little check-ins, but I feel as though I'm on trial.

"So…" I begin stiltedly, "What's the diagnosis, Dr.?"

Gary folds his hand over his slight paunch, leaning back in his chair and appraising me.

"You've been getting glowing reviews from the other instructors," he tells me point-blank, "They've been very impressed with your work so far, Sophie. Your acting teacher, Karen Krause, is particularly interested in you."

I sit up a little straighter in my chair. Karen Krause is one of our guest artists this summer. Back in New York, she's the artistic director of one of the city's most exciting experimental theatre companies. Being in her good graces is a huge deal.

"This isn't exactly public information," Gary goes on, "But Karen isn't just here as an instructor this summer. She's scouting the eight of you Sheridan kids for a spot in her apprentice company this coming fall. If accepted, you'd be living in New York for at least a year. You could get school credit for taking part and meet your graduation requirements on the other side of the country. It would be an incredible opportunity. And Karen has told me that you, above all the other students, are the person she has in mind for the spot."

My jaw falls open as I struggle to comprehend what Gary is telling me. I can feel my mind rebelling against the information, because it seems far too good to be true. Living in New York City, working with a professional theatre company, all while finishing up my degree here at Sheridan? That would be absolutely perfect. Maybe Anna could even come live with me? God knows, New York is a dream for any photographer...

My fanciful daydreaming grinds to a halt as I take in the look on Gary's face. He's practically grimacing at me.

"Isn't this...good news?" I ask him tentatively, "Why do you look like you want to drop kick me out of your office?"

"I'm...concerned. About you," Gary goes on measuredly, his fingers steepled against his lips.

"Why?" I ask, cocking my head, "I'm doing fine, Gary. You just said, all the other instructors are happy with my work. What's the problem?"

"I did say that all the *other* instructors were happy with you," Gary prods.

"...But not you," I reply, disappointed.

"Not me," Gary goes on, "Over the past three years, I've gotten to see you grow immensely as a performer. You came to me as an angry, closed off little girl with no interest in connecting to anyone. But you've worked like mad to open up, let other people in, be vulnerable. You're far from perfect as a performer. You're unpredictable at times, you've got some bad habits to shake, but what I love about you is that you're honest. You're raw, and messy, and real. At least, you *were.* Up until a few weeks ago."

"I...I don't understand," I murmur, looking down at my hands.

"Something has changed in you, since you've been away," Gary says with frank honesty, "Don't get me wrong, you're still a perfectly competent performer. The best in your class, even. You've shown great technical skill these past couple of weeks, everything by the book, on point. But you know something, Sophie? Perfect isn't you. Safe isn't you. And I worry that if people start rewarding you for the work you're doing now, with apprenticeships and praise and whatever, you'll stop growing. And if you stop growing, I'm afraid you'll never become as great a performer as you have the potential to be."

"Are you just saying this because you want me to stay here in Montana?" I ask hopefully.

"You know I'd never try to keep you here out of selfishness," Gary says firmly, "I know this is all difficult to hear, but I need you to listen to me now. It's not too late for you to course correct, here. You've thrown up the defenses around your heart again since you've been gone, but that doesn't mean you have to keep them up forever. I don't know what's happening in your life, or what has you so scared, but you need to face it, Sophie. And soon."

Hot tears prick at my eyes as I look away from my teacher. He's seen right through me, as usual. Why did I think I could hide anything from him?

"What if…I'm not strong enough to face it?" I ask him softly, "I've only just barely started working through what's already happened to me, to my family…I'm afraid that if I let myself get hurt again, I'll be back to square one."

"What do we always say around here, Sophie?" Gary says, "Follow the fear…"

"…If you want to find the truth," I finish, blinking back my tears.

He's right, of course. I've been barreling along, refusing to deal with what's happened between me and Luke. Refusing to deal with the loss of him, just like I refused to deal with losing my dad at first. It's a different sort of loss, but no less real. And no less destructive, if left unchecked.

"You can do this, Sophie," Gary goes on, "You owe it to yourself to chase down the truth. That's the only way you're ever really going to be happy."

I know whose lead to follow, if I want to find my truth. The problem is, I have no idea where to find him.

I offer Gary a murmured goodbye and hurry out of the office. My cheeks are flushed with embarrassment at being called out by my favorite teacher. I've disappointed him, and disappointed myself. I thought I was doing such a good job at moving on from Luke, but all I've really been doing is shutting out any passing thought of him. I've been holding my need of him at bay, denying how much his departure really hurt me. And it's only now that I realize how exhausted I've become with the effort.

Bursting out of the performing arts building, I gulp down huge swallows of fresh air, trying to keep my tears at bay. But it's no use. I stumble forward, steadying myself against a park bench overlooking the grassy Sheridan lawns as I give into my sadness at last. My shoulders shake as I sink down onto the bench, burying my face in my hands. Warm July sunlight kisses my bare shoulders, but I only feel a numb chill. I have to face the facts—I've completely messed up any chance at being with Luke. Why didn't I just tell him the truth, when he left me here that night? Why didn't I say that I wanted him to stay, no matter what? For someone so allergic to bullshit, I've sure been doling out my fair share of it lately.

I jump as my cell starts to chime in my purse. Sniffling morosely, I dig the device out and check the caller ID. It's Maddie. I let out a huge sigh, sinking back against the bench. Maddie only ever calls me for two reasons—in case of family emergency, or to complain about Mom. And to be honest, I'm hardly in the mood for either just now. But then again, this is the first time I've had an actual call from either of my sisters in weeks. The most I've gotten are vague, perfunctory texts. I can't ignore this.

"H-hey Maddie," I say, picking up the call, "What's up?"

"Hey Sophie…Are you OK?" my big sister replies over the line, "You sound like you're coming down with something."

"No, no," I say quickly, my voice thickening. The one surefire way to get me crying is to give me an opening by asking what's wrong. I try and outrun the next wave of tears, but it's no use.

"Soph, what's the matter?" Maddie asks softly, as I try and stifle my sobs, "What's going on?"

"It's st-stupid," I blubber, thanking my lucky stars that the campus is nearly empty. I'd be quite the sight to come upon right now. "Don't worry about it."

"I can't not worry," Maddie tells me, "You're my little sister. Did something happen at school? Is it a guy? Is it a family thing?"

A little bit of all three, I think sullenly.

"Whatever it is, you know you can talk to me, right?" Maddie presses on, "I know we haven't always been super close, but this has been such a crazy couple of weeks. And I... I don't think there's anyone else in the world who can understand what we're going through right now except each other. We Porter women have to stick together at times like this."

I bite my lip, leaving my sister hanging on the line. With the way everything imploded at the lake house, I almost forgot that Luke and I were getting ready to let our secret slip to our siblings. It would be such a relief to tell Maddie about what's been going on. And now that Luke has ghosted out of my life, what's the point in keeping our secret for another second?

"Sophie? Are you still there?" Maddie asks.

"Yeah. Sorry. I was just...It's kind of a long story," I tell her, shoving a hand through my hair.

"It's OK. I'm listening," she assures me.

"Well..." I begin as my heart jackhammers in my chest, "I guess you could say that I'm having a spot of guy trouble. And not just any guy, either. I... Christ, this is going to sound insane—"

"Sophie," Maddie cuts in gently, "Is the guy Luke?"

My jaw falls into my lap at my sister's words.

"I—What—How did you—?" I sputter.

"Holy crap," she breathes, "Cash was right!"

"Cash? What does Cash have to do with anything?" I demand, leaping to my feet, "And how did you know about—?"

"Cash was totally onto you guys by the time we left the lake house. And I have to say, I had my suspicions too," Maddie tells me, "You could barely look at him without blushing. So, what's the real story Soph?"

I'm too stunned to deny anything. "Luke wasn't just some guy I'd seen around Sheridan," I tell my sister, "He was my TA this past semester. I sort of had a thing for him the whole time he was my teacher. And…Uh…The feeling was mutual."

"That is so much juicer than what I imagined," Maddie says excitedly, "Go on!"

"Okay…" I continue, "Well, right after the semester ended, we sort of hooked up."

"What!"

"…In a bar bathroom."

"*What*?!"

"And the only reason we didn't get it on right then and there is because Luke had to save me and my best friend from getting beat up by a bunch of skinheads."

"WHAT?!"

"So, yeah," I go on, "We were already sort of a thing before I left for the lake house. But I had no idea until I got there that Luke was John's son. We were both completely blindsided. And we just… Thought it would be better to keep it a secret, and just pick up once we were back at Sheridan. So we just spent the week sneaking around, trying not to get caught."

"Your sneaking could use some work," Maddie tells me.

"I'm getting that, yeah," I laugh wryly, "But I mean, it's not like it even matters now.

"Why not?"

"What do you mean, 'why not'?" I shoot back, "Because of Mom and John. Their choice to shack up for good totally ruined any chance Luke and I had of picking things up when we got back here. We both thought for sure they'd break up, but instead Mom gets a set of keys to the place? Now, instead of spending the summer with Luke, I'm just here licking my wounds on my own—"

"Wait. I don't understand. Luke isn't with you?" Maddie asks.

"Of course not," I tell her, "He dropped me off at campus and split. It's not like we could just pretend like everything was OK and stay together like a normal couple."

"But…It sounds like that's exactly what you want to do," Maddie points out.

"Sure, in a perfect world," I scoff.

"You don't have to laugh it off," she tells me, "It's not ridiculous."

"I'm sorry…Were you not there for the part where his dad and our mom are an item?" I reply, "In what universe is it OK for us to go on—"

"Man, and here I thought you were supposed to be the free-loving hippie in the family," Maddie laughs, "How am *I* the one telling *you* not to be a prude now?"

"That's…a very good question," I say slowly, planting a hand on my hip, "Why aren't you freaking out about all this? The Maddie I know would be telling me I'm a perverted sex fiend right now. What the hell gives?"

Maddie sighs on the other end of the line.

"Let's just say…I kind of know what you're going through," she tells me.

"Wh-what?" I stammer. "What do you…?"

And then it hits me. The scene I witnessed that last night at the lake, when the pickup drove off leaving a devastated Maddie in its dust. I thought she was just upset about Mom's behavior, and our house getting sold off, but really…

"*No,*" I breathe.

"Yeah," Maddie replies.

"You and Cash?!" I gasp, "You two were… But how is that—?"

"It's also something of a long story," she tells me, "But it involves a one-night stand at a roadside motel, if you can believe it."

"Madeleine Porter, who *are* you even?" I ask, mind reeling.

"Someone who knows a thing or two about what you're grappling with," she tells me.

I sink back down on the bench, landing heavily. How did I not pick up on the fact that Maddie and Cash had a thing for each other? And here I thought *I* was the actress of the family. There's also the fact that Cash is the last person I could ever picture my sister with. She's always gone for boring, bland, safe guys. Bad boy, punch-throwing Cash Hawthorne is anything *but* safe. I guess I was so wrapped up in my own drama with Luke that I didn't even think for a second about anyone else at that house. God, what else have I been missing?

"How are you so calm, then?" I ask Maddie, "Shouldn't you be just as broken up about this whole thing as I am? I mean, to be forced to call off your thing with Cash because—"

"That's the thing, Sophie," Maddie cuts in, "We haven't called anything off. We're still very much together."

"…What."

"I was totally freaked out about Mom and John too, at first," Maddie tells me, "I bailed on Cash, told him I couldn't keep seeing him if our parents' relationship was getting serious. I tried to go back to Seattle and get on with my life. But I couldn't. I was miserable without him."

"So…What did you do?"

"Luckily, I have a little guardian angel out here with me in Seattle. Or, maybe a guardian devil? My best friend Allie, the one who works at ReImaged with me? She arranged for Cash to be hired by our firm for a PR project we're working on now. He's one of our 'everyman models' for this denim campaign we're running."

"Cash is a model?!" I ask, unable to keep from laughing.

"I know. It's insane," Maddie laughs too, "Honestly, it's kind of just a cover. A reason for him to be in Seattle with me while we figure out how to go forward. As a couple. Of course, now we're hiding our relationship from our employers *and* our parents…"

"But not your baby sister," I point out.

"No. And I'm glad," Maddie says, her voice taking on a serious cast, "I'm glad that you told me about you and Luke, too. Because now, for perhaps the first time in my life, I can give you some big-sisterly advice. You listening?"

"Oh, I'm all ears."

"If breaking things off with Luke is what you really want, then I'm certainly not going to try and talk you out of it. But if you don't mind my saying so, it doesn't sound like you want him out of your life. It sounds to me like you're scared."

"Scared?" I say, clutching the phone to my ear, "Scared of what?"

"Scared of what people will think. Scared that you're doing something sick or wrong. Scared that you're setting yourself up for heartbreak. Need I go on?"

"No…" I whisper, "No, that's about the size of it."

"I don't mean to sound all high and mighty. I still don't have my own feelings for Cash all the way figured out. I mean, they're still…What did Anna say? Our 'almost brothers'?"

"Ugh. Don't remind me," I groan.

"But that *almost* is the important part," Maddie urges, "Last time I checked, we don't share a drop of blood with the Hawthorne boys. And I didn't see any ring on Mom's finger. There's nothing wrong with what you feel for Luke. Nothing."

"Even though our parents are together? Christ, even though you and Cash—?"

"Let's be honest for a second, Soph," Maddie cuts in, "Since when has our family functioned in anything approaching a normal way? How much has Mom even been involved in your life these past few years? God, to what extent has she ever even acted like a mother to us?"

"She's not perfect," I allow, "But it's like you said yourself, back at the lake. Family's not something you can ever forget."

"No," Maddie allows, "We'll never forget the place she had in our lives when we were small. And we'll always, always love her. But she's moved on from the part of her life that included us. She said as much herself. And if she's written off her past..."

"Then why can't we," I say softly, feeling the world come into focus around me.

"We've already been robbed of our happiness once in our lives," Maddie says firmly, "Losing Dad nearly destroyed us all. Maybe a new start is what all of us Porter women need. Even if that means going our own ways. God knows, we kind of already have."

I sit silently, taking in everything Maddie's said to me. For the first time in weeks, I feel the faintest flutter of hope coming back to life inside me. Maybe it's crazy to go along with what she's saying. Maybe I'm just clinging onto her words because they give me a shot at having a future with Luke. But maybe it doesn't matter...Maybe all that matters is keeping that little flare of hope alive, nursing it until it erupts into full blown happiness.

It's certainly worth a shot.

"You're not too bad at this big sister thing," I finally say, my voice hoarse with emotion.

"Gee. Thanks," Maddie drawls.

"Thank *you*. Seriously," I whisper.

"Of course," she says softly, "I'm so glad you told me what was going on with you. Not least of all because I have an idea."

"An idea about what?" I ask her.

"About how to get you and Luke back together, of course," she tells me.

"Whoa, whoa. Slow your roll, sister," I tell her.

"No time to waste, Sophie. Do you want this boy back in your life or not?"

"I...I do," I tell her.

Saying it out loud, I know at once that it's the truth. I want Luke to be a part of my life again. Whatever it takes. Even if it means trusting my romantic life to my lapsed-prude of a sister.

"Well OK then," she says. I can practically hear her grinning across the state line, "Here's what I'm thinking..."

Chapter Thirteen

Maddie's master plan boils down to this: getting Luke and I back in the same place and letting fate take its course. Her agency, ReImaged, is hosting a big party to launch their campaign for Asphalt denim. Cash will be there as a "brand ambassador" and Maddie is pretty much running the whole show with her wily coworker Allie. Maddie will get my name on the guest list to the exclusive event, and make sure that Cash invites Luke as well. Once Luke and I cross paths at the party, the ball will be in my court. I'll have to find a way to convince him to give us a chance, despite the odds. Whether or not I can do that is anyone's guess.

But I have to take the shot. Surely, Luke will be able to understand *that.*

The only real hitch in Maddie's scheme is that the Asphalt party is tomorrow night. In Seattle. A full day's drive from Sheridan University. Which is a pretty daunting obstacle, seeing as I don't currently have a car. Daunting, but not insurmountable.

The second I get off the phone with Maddie, I race across campus to Danny's dorm room. Time is of the essence if I'm going to pull this off, and I'm going to need to call in every favor I've got (and even a few that I *haven't* got). I charge into Danny's building, take the stairs two at a time, and nearly body slam his door as I skid to a halt before it.

"Danny!" I call, hammering the door with my fist, "Danny, are you home?"

The door swings open, but it isn't Danny who greets me. For a second, I have trouble placing the attractive, dark haired man standing in my best friend's doorway. But he recognizes me right away.

"Hey Maddie!" he smiles, pulling me into a hug.

"Oh, hey!" I reply giving him a friendly pat on the back.

"I haven't seen you since that dreadful night at The Bear Trap," he goes on excitedly, "How have you been doing?"

That's where I know him from. It's Greg—the guy Danny was chatting up the night I hooked up with Luke at the bar. The guy who came and fetched us just before Danny got jumped by those assholes. Looks like their flirtation wasn't just a one-night thing, either.

"I've been...OK," I tell him, "Some family drama. A dash of guy trouble."

"Sounds like quite the summer," Greg nods.

"Indeed," I reply, "Hey, is Danny here? It's kind of urgent."

On cue, my best friend appears in the bathroom doorway, a towel wrapped around his sculpted hips. He stops in his tracks as he catches sight of me and Greg chatting at the door. I've never seen my brash, confident friend look bashful before. What gives?

"Heyyy, Sophie," Danny says slowly, adjusting his towel, "What brings you here?"

"Well," I tell him, "There's been a pretty interesting development in the Luke saga, and I may need your help. Scratch that, I definitely need your help."

"Wait, wait," Greg cuts in, "This sounds like the beginning of an adventure. And that calls for something fermented. Give me one sec."

He dashes off into the kitchen, and I raise an eyebrow at Danny.

"So you get to know every detail of my love life, but I don't hear a word about this?"

"Ugh. I was just...too embarrassed to tell you, OK?" Danny sighs, "I mean, seeing the same person for more than a week? I'm getting so *boring*."

"I think it's sweet," I tell him, "You guys seem happy."

"So far, so good," Danny allows, "Who would have thought I'd meet such a nice boy at a backwoods biker bar?"

"Stranger things have happened," I shrug, "And speaking of, wait until I tell you what's going on with my sister. Put some pants on. This may take a while to explain…"

Once all present are fully dressed and furnished with glasses of rosé, I sit Danny and Greg down to fill them in on my predicament. Greg's jaw inches slowly toward the floor as I get him up to speed, and Danny's follows suit when I reveal Maddie's secret affair with Cash.

"And no 'all in the family' jokes just yet," I warn them, taking a big sip of wine, "There's more."

I tell the boys about Maddie's plan to get me face-to-face with Luke again, and about ReImaged's Asphalt launch party in Seattle tomorrow. Their eyes go wide as I describe the event as Maddie did on the phone. The party is going down in a newly renovated industrial warehouse turned luxury hotel on the Seattle waterfront. All of the "everyman models" featured in Asphalt's new ad campaign will be present. This is the launch of the company's brand new men's line, so they're not cutting any corners.

"So there's going to be booze, beautiful men, and a spur-of-the-moment road trip?" Danny asks me, sounding like a little kid at Christmas.

"My only question is, where are our invites?" Greg grins.

"I'd be more than happy to have some moral support," I tell them, "And…even happier if one of you would be willing to chip in some wheels."

"We can take my car," Greg says decisively.

"Really?" I ask with bated breath, "You'd haul some girl you've barely met across state lines, just like that?"

"Any friend of Daniel's is a friend of mine," Greg says warmly, "I'd be happy to help."

Daniel? I mouth to my best friend as Greg takes a swig of wine.

Shut up, he mouths back, unable to hide his smile.

"Next question," Greg goes on, setting down his glass, "When do we leave?"

"Um…Right now, more or less," I say nervously.

"No time like the present," Danny says, rising to his feet, "You go pack up, Soph. We'll come get you in twenty. And be sure to pack your sexiest underthings. We're not dragging you all the way to Seattle just so you can horrify Professor Sexy Pants with your granny panties."

"Hey. Granny panties are making a comeback," I tell him, "The internet says so."

"Ugh," Danny shudders, "All the more reason never to go near technology.

I give him a quick kiss on the cheek. "Thank you. Both of you. You're really saving me, here."

"It's not every day you get to be an accessory to an epic lovers' reunion," Gary says.

"We don't even know how he's going to react," I say cautiously. "He could be furious to find me at this party, for all we know."

"He's going to be thrilled," Greg assures me, "I just know it."

The certainty of a near-stranger will have to do for now. I turn on my heel and dart out of the room, off to pack my bags for the adventure—or the disappointment—of a lifetime.

It isn't just any set of wheels that Gary donates to the cause of reuniting me and Luke. The boys swing around to pick me up in a vintage BMW convertible. The top is down, the radio is blasting, and the engine is running.

"Is this for real?" I laugh, tossing my bag into the backseat and hopping in after it.

"You better believe it's real," Danny calls back, "How's this for a chariot, m'lady?"

We take off in the late afternoon sunlight, bidding adieu to Sheridan for the next few days. By the time I lay eyes on this place again come Monday, my life will be inalterably changed. It's just hard to say in which direction.

But as the three of us peel off onto the open road, singing along to Nicki Minaj at the top of our lungs, I feel my reservations begin to melt away. Whatever happens in Seattle, I will have gone after my happiness at full speed. And that's all one can do, in the end.

We spend the night in the cheapest (and seediest) roadside motel we can find along the way. The blue-haired woman that checks us in nearly has a heart attack when we request a single room.

"Are you one of those open marriages, or what have you?" she asks us, clearly appalled.

"Would you refuse to let us stay here if we were?" I ask.

"I have the right to refuse anyone a room," the old woman huffs, crossing her meaty arms, "I don't like unconventional arrangements."

"There's nothing unconventional about us," Danny says, flashing her a winning smile. That grin would work on anyone.

The receptionist relents, sliding a plastic key card across the counter.

"Well, if you say so…" she purrs, charmed by my sandy-haired BFF.

"Thanks, sweetheart," Danny replies, snatching up the key and turning away.

The second all our backs are turned, Danny slips and arm around Greg's waist. I have to swallow a laugh as I hear the blue-haired woman *harrumph* behind us.

"If only she knew we were bringing you to reunite with your stepbrother-professor-lover," Danny remarks over his shoulder, "That would *really* get her blood boiling."

"Maybe you can start keeping that little detail to yourself, huh Danny?" I suggest, punching him in the shoulder. "I hardly want that to be the headline of our relationship.

"Sorry," he shrugs, "I can't help it if taboos are sexy as hell. And I'm pretty sure you two are gunning for the record of taboos-per-relationship."

"Great," I mutter, trailing them across the motel parking lot, "Something to tell the grandkids."

***

By late afternoon the following day, we finally start seeing signs for the city of Seattle. This place is sometimes called the Emerald City, and I certainly feel like Dorothy right now—hoping that my every wish will be fulfilled by this bustling new metropolis. Of course, Danny and Greg are far better company than any Tin Man or Scarecrow.

"Holy shit," Danny whistles, as our destination comes into sight, "This place is *incredible*."

And indeed, it is. Maddie was not exaggerating when she said ReImaged booked the coolest new spot in Seattle for the Asphalt launch party. The venue is a sprawling, ornate old factory space, entirely renovated as a swanky, industrial chic hotel. All of the original architecture has been preserved and perfected with stunning interior design. Elegant copper touches, Edison bulb chandeliers, and eye-catching works of modern art elevate the space from edgy to masterfully wrought.

A valet takes the BMW off our hands, and our motley trio is left on the curb, gaping up at the hotel. I'm never stepped foot in a place half as fancy as this. I'm suddenly self-conscious of my grubby backpack and yoga pants.

"Sophie!" I hear a familiar voice call from within the hotel.

I look up to see Maddie hurrying toward me. She's rocking tall black heels, a bright red pencil skirt, and a silky white blouse. I've never seen my big sister in work mode. I have to say, I'm impressed.

"I'm so glad you're here," she beams, wrapping me up in a big hug.

I hug her fiercely back, happier to see her than ever. I didn't realize until this second, but I really need my big sister right now.

"And you've brought an entourage," Maddie observes, looking over at my friends.

"Oh, right!" I say, "Maddie, this is my friend Danny."

"Of course, I've heard all about you," Maddie says to my best friend, shaking his hand.

"Ditto," grins, "Though Sophie never mentioned that you were a stone cold fox."

"Easy tiger," Greg mutters, "You already have a date for the dance, remember?"

"This is Greg," Danny tells Maddie, "My chaperone."

"Very nice to meet you both," Maddie says, shaking Greg's hand. "Come on inside and let me show you around! I hope you don't mind, I may have gone a little overboard with your accommodations."

This turns out to be the understatement of the century.

Maddie managed to snag a few of the hotel's exclusive deluxe rooms at the last minute. Greg and Danny are happy to share, and peel off to get settled straightaway. Maddie and I are on our own as she leads me down the hall to my own room.

"Here we are," Maddie says excitedly, swinging open the door. I step past her over the threshold and feel the wind rush out of my lungs.

This isn't a room at all. It's a *suite*. A palatial living room opens up before me, expertly decorated with a midcentury modern flare. A wide balcony overlooks the water, and I spot a heavenly queen bed and full bathroom through a door to my left. The kitchen is stocked with a full wine rack and—be still my heart—a professional grade espresso machine.

"Maddie…" I breathe, slowly spinning around at the center of the room. "This…This is…"

"Can't blame a girl for spoiling her little sister once in a while," Maddie grins, "Especially when that little sister's been having a helluva few weeks."

"Somehow, I feel like those few weeks are about to be overridden," I tell her, "And it's all thanks to you."

"Hey, don't thank me yet," Maddie cautions, "I'm just getting your lover boy here. You have to do all the real work. Although, I have a few more presents that may help the effort along."

"*More* presents?" I laugh, "What are you—?"

"Look in the closet," Maddie says, bouncing excitedly on the balls of her feet.

I make my way into the bedroom and ease open the closet. Hanging on the closet door is the sexiest little red dress I've ever seen. The lush, structured material is of the highest quality, and the ultra-low back is absolutely breathtaking. With the sky-high gold stilettos sitting in their box on the closet floor, this is the most high-end ensemble I've ever seen up close.

"Is this…for me?" I ask Maddie, dumbfounded.

"That it is," she smiles, "It's all from Asphalt's latest women's line. I hope you don't mind, but I had to list you as a brand ambassador to snag this suite. So technically, you're here representing the company tonight. I figured you wouldn't mind putting in a night of event modeling."

"Not if it means I get to wear this when Luke sees me again," I laugh, gingerly touching the exquisite dress. "Are you sure you're not actually my fairy godmother instead of my sister?"

"It's the least I can do," Maddie tells me, "After what we've both been through, we deserve a little magic, don't you think?"

"Sounds about right to me," I say, taking her hand in mine. "How have you been doing out here since you got back?"

"Pretty great, actually," she says, walking me over to the cloud-like queen bed, "Ever since Cash got here, that is."

"It's still so hard for me to picture you guys as a couple," I say, shaking my head, "Opposites attract, I guess."

"Porters and Hawthornes attract, apparently," she laughs wryly. "I wouldn't exactly expect you and Luke to pair off, either. The upstanding, super star athlete and the rebellious, snarky artist?"

"I know, I know," I sigh, "But there's a whole lot more to Luke than his golden-boy veneer, I'll say that much."

"There's more to Cash than his tatted-up bad boy act too," she nods, "Who knows? Maybe even John has a hidden self beneath that abusive asshole thing."

"Ugh. Let's not talk about John Hawthorne. Preferably ever," I scowl.

"Deal," Maddie replies, "Besides, there's no more time for small talk. We need to get you ready."

Chapter Fourteen

I can feel the bass line of roaring rock music even before I reach the ground floor. Each pounding beat vibrates up through my spike-heeled feet, sending shivers of anticipation down my bare back. I smooth down the front of my skin-tight red dress and give my artfully tousled hair a shake. I'm far more accustomed to dance clothes than body-con, but any self-consciousness I may feel is totally trumped by sheer nerves.

This is it, I think to myself as the elevator doors whisper open, *Moment of truth.*

Drawing back my shoulders, I stride confidently forward with as much swagger as I can muster...and promptly smack into a solid wall of leather-clad muscle. I very nearly tumble over in my sky high stilettos before a firm hand catches me by the elbow, pulling me to standing. The first glance of my aide's familiar profile sets my head spinning dizzily. For a second, I could swear it was Luke who just kept me from sprawling across the carpet. But upon second glance, I see that's not quite right...

"What're you, drunk already?" Cash grins, letting go of my arm.

"No, but that's not a bad idea," I grumble, shaking off my near-spill. "What're you doing out here? Shouldn't you be strutting your stuff on the catwalk or something?"

"Maddie sent me out to wait for you," Cash replies coolly, ignoring my jab, "She thought we should make our entrance together."

I appraise Luke's big brother, decked out from head to toe in pieces from Asphalt's new line of menswear. I've said it before and I'll say it again—Cash Hawthorne is easy on the eyes. Not my type at all, but with just enough of a resemblance to Luke to make our stint as Mr. and Mrs. Asphalt Denim pretty weird. Especially now that I know he and my sister are an item.

"I know," Cash shrugs, reading my mind, "The four of us are gonna make for one pretty fucked up double date tonight, huh?"

"So Luke is coming, then?" I ask excitedly, hurrying after Cash as he turns for the ballroom.

"Sure is," he replies, shooting a glance my way, "And also, I have to say...*called it*. Your little secret was no match for this big brother."

"Yeah, yeah," I mutter, rolling my eyes, "You're a real super sleuth, Cash."

"Just glad I could be of service, reuniting you with your Casanova," he replies, "I'm actually sort of surprised I got a hold of him at all. Sounds like he's been off on something of a spirit quest."

I imagine Luke roaming off on his own, trying to make sense of the hand fate has dealt us. What if he's already sorted out his conflicted confusion? Landed on a solution that doesn't involve me? I guess I'll find out soon enough.

"Here we are," Cash says, stopping before an impenetrable-looking set of steel double doors.

"Ready?" I ask him, squaring my shoulders.

"Are *you*?" he shoots back.

"Not even remotely," I laugh, "But what choice do we have now?"

Cash makes a big show of offering me his arm, but I take it gratefully all the same. I could use the extra support as I get ready to face Luke again after three long weeks that have felt even longer. Together, Cash and I step forward and push open the heavy metallic doors. A wall of music and light hits me square on as I step across the threshold. The dizzying array of sensation swallows me whole, and the only thing I know for sure is that I won't emerge from this event unchanged.

It's almost absurd to call this place a hotel ballroom. It's more like a gutted and glamorized factory floor, all exposed brick and smooth concrete studded with sleek fixtures and minimalist furniture. A stunning glass and copper chandelier hangs overhead, with tons of Edison bulb lanterns lighting the rest of the space. Cash's face is plastered everywhere, along with the faces of Asphalt's other "everyman models". But there's only one man I have any interest in laying eyes on right now...And he's nowhere to be seen.

Cash and I make our way to the heart of the party, turning heads with every step we take. The pounding hard rock music provided by the live band doesn't quite drown out the murmurs that follow in our wake. If only these gawking guests knew the true nature of my and Cash's relationship. Then they'd really have something to talk about.

"There you are!" I hear Danny call out from the long steel bar running along one side of the room. He and Greg grab their martini glasses and rush over to me and Cash, eyes agog.

"You look incredible!" Greg breathes, taking in my ensemble.

"You two don't clean up too badly yourselves," I reply, noting their artfully distressed denim and slick jackets.

"And who's your escort?" Danny asks, raising an eyebrow at Cash.

"Oh, this is Cash," I tell them, "Luke's brother."

"And the man of the hour, I see..." Greg observes, looking around at the larger than life projections of Cash's face all over the room.

"That's me," Cash laughs, shaking my friends' hands, "I've gone from ex-military mechanic to model matchmaker in three weeks flat. These Porter women will do a number on you."

"By 'do a number' you mean 'make your life infinitely better', right?" I hear Maddie say as she appears at Cash's shoulder with an adorable redheaded woman at her side.

"Holy crap," the redhead says, catching a glimpse of me, "You're Sophie? Maddie's little sister?"

"Guilty," I tell her.

"You're *stunning*," she gushes, laying a hand on her ample chest, "I'm Allie, by the way."

"My own personal bad influence," Maddie tells me.

"Well, it looks like the gang's all here," Cash says, looking around at our little circle.

"Almost…" I murmur, glancing anxiously around the room. Still no sign of Luke that I can see. What if he's changed his mind about coming?

"He'll be here, Soph," Maddie says, taking my arm and leading me toward the bar. "Come on. Brand ambassadors drink free."

"That is a mighty dangerous offer," I laugh, "But it's certainly not one I'm going to turn down. Not tonight."

I drink down my liquid courage and hit the dance floor with Greg and Danny, determined to look every bit the breezy free spirit I don't exactly feel like at the moment. Still, my mood can't help but be lifted by the rocking music, dashing company, and complementary liquor. By the time an hour has gone by, I'm hardly faking my enthusiasm at all—even if Luke has blown way past the point of being fashionably late.

I'm sandwiched between Greg and Danny, bumping and grinding like my life depends on it, when I catch a glimpse of Maddie flagging me down from the edge of the dance floor.

"Soph!" she yells over the blaring music. "Come here a sec!"

"Nooo, you're gonna throw off my groove!" I crow, twerking ridiculously in her direction.

"Are you gonna make me drag you off the floor?" she presses, planting her hands on her hips.

"Ugh. Fine," I pout dramatically, picking my way through the crowd to her side. I grab a glass of champagne off a passing tray as I stop in front of my sister. "What is it?"

"I want to show you something," she says, grabbing my wrist and towing me across the room.

"What?" I ask, struggling to keep up on my staggering heels.

"The, uh, view from the terrace," she says bobbing and weaving through the crowd.

"It's the same view from my room," I protest, "Come on. How am I supposed to drink and dance my nerves away if you keep—?"

"It's just through here!" Maddie goes on, stopping in front of a frosted glass door. I'm surprised to find Cash and Allie waiting there for us, too. They're both wearing wide, knowing smiles as I approach with Maddie.

"What is this, a field trip?" I ask.

"Not exactly," my sister says, taking me by the shoulders, "We just wanted to give you two some moral support."

"You...two?" I breathe, heart leaping into my throat.

"That's right," Maddie smiles, nodding at Cash and Allie to open the doors, "Enjoy the view."

And with that, my sister grabs my champagne flute and gives me a gentle shove through the doorway. I step out into the warm July night, a granite terrace stretching out before me under a canopy of white string lights. I'm sure that the waterfront view is absolutely stunning in the gathering twilight, but I can't say for sure. My gaze has been arrested by a sight that's far more breathtaking.

His form is backlit by the wide expanse of sky and sea beyond the terrace. That familiar shape I've come to know so well—from memorizing the feel of it, and feeling the hole it left in my life upon departing—is here once more. Close enough to touch, but only if I dare.

Hearing the door close behind me, Luke glances up across the space, turning his face my way. His eyes alight on me, and I feel my body come alive under his gaze. It's as though I've just woken up for the first time in weeks, but only to find myself in the middle of a fabulous dream.

"I hope you don't mind my cutting in," Luke says, his voice rich and full as it draws me across the terrace, "But I didn't think this was a moment that should go down on the dance floor."

He stands there in a perfectly cut charcoal suit, his hands tucked into his pockets. His chestnut hair is a bit longer than when we last met, its slight wave pushed back away from his sculpted face. Those green eyes that memorized every inch of me just weeks ago shine like lighthouse beacons now, filling me with hope that my days being lost at sea are over.

"You're here," I say softly, drawing to a stop within paces of him.

"You sound surprised," he says, taking a swinging step toward me.

"I just...I wasn't sure. I guess I was afraid to hope I'd see you here," I breathe.

"Well, once I had official marching orders from your sister, there was no backing out," he says, the corners of his lips lifting.

"Oh god," I laugh nervously, wishing I still had a drink in my hand, "I hope you weren't manhandled into coming here tonight."

"Are you kidding?" he replies, raking his eyes down along my form, "Once I knew you'd be here, nothing could have stopped me."

"But...You knew where I was, Luke," I say, "I was right where you left me. All these weeks...You could have just come back if you wanted to see me again. I thought—"

"It's not as simple as that," Luke says, his brow furrowing, "I couldn't have just stayed in that place, Sophie."

"Why not?" I ask softly, clasping my hands, "Why did you have to leave, just like that?"

His mouth straightens into a hard line. No amount of engineering by our siblings could have made this a seamless, perfect reunion. There's too much we need to work out. Too many grievances to air. But I'll stay out here all night if I have to. I won't risk another word going unsaid between us.

"That place, Sheridan, is a part of my past," Luke begins slowly, turning to look out across the water, "The person I was there—the brochure-perfect track star, the MBA-grubbing suit—that's not the person I really am. Just like I'm not the responsible, family-man of a son that I'm forced to be in my hometown. After everything that happened to us that last night at the lake, I needed to go some place where I could find out which version of me is the honest one."

"And did you?" I ask, taking a small step forward.

"I did," Luke murmurs, swinging his gaze toward me, "But not during these past few weeks. I realized I'd already found it. I found it the first time we were alone together. When I finally met someone that didn't need me to be anything different—anything *more* than I am."

"I sure as hell hope you're talking about me," I whisper, heart pounding, "Otherwise this is going to be awkward as fuck..."

"Of course it's you, Sophia," Luke laughs roughly, grabbing hold of my hand and tugging me toward him, "It's been you this whole time. I was too much of a fucking idiot to see it."

"At any other point these past few weeks, I would have agreed with you…" I laugh, resting my hands on the panes of his chest, "But I'm having trouble being even the slightest bit mad at you right now, to be honest."

"Oh no," he grins down at me, circling his hands around my cinched waist, "Does that mean makeup sex is off the table?"

"Why don't you kiss me and we'll find out together?" I say, lacing my fingers behind his neck.

Luke lifts a hand to my chin and tilts my face toward his, beneath the twinkling string lights.

"I feel like we're in one of those shitty teen movies," he laughs, shaking his head.

"Well, that just won't do," I reply, pressing my body to his.

"Hold on," he says, glancing over my shoulder, "I've got it…"

I gasp as Luke grabs hold of my hips and lifts me effortlessly off the ground. I circle my arms around his shoulders, my caramel hair falling across my face as Luke strides across the terrace. The coarse brush of brick against the bare skin of my back makes me shudder with delight as Luke presses me up against the warehouse wall. I hook one leg around his waist, letting my dress slip dangerously high as he lowers me down, pressing his perfect body to mine. My eyes flutter closed as he pins me to the wall with his hips, letting me feel the glorious length of him pressed up against my thigh.

"That's better," he growls, running his hands down my smooth sides.

"Much," I breathe, catching his face in my hands.

His mouth finds mine in the shadow of the warehouse, and I fall open to him as I have so many times before. I bury my fingers in his chestnut hair as his tongue sweeps against mine. The taste and smell of him bombard my senses, filling me with such longing and relief that I nearly lose it right there. Not until this moment have I let myself confront just how much I've missed him, missed *this*.

"I fucking hated leaving you," Luke growls, kissing down along my bare throat as he grinds his hips against mine, "But I have to say, I'm a big fan of coming back."

"Then we'd better make this reunion count," I laugh, running a hand along that staggering desire testing the strength of his slacks, "Because the leaving part nearly killed me."

"I'll make it up to you," Luke vows, suddenly serious as his green eyes lock on mine, "Trust me when I say that I will."

"Well, I know a pretty good way you can start," I grin back at him, feeling him growing harder in my hands.

"Oh, that's a given," he smiles back, his eyes closing as he savors my touch, "But aren't you on the clock, Miss Asphalt Denim?"

"I'm sure I can take a fifteen," I say, my voice dipping low as I bring my hands to Luke's belt buckle, "Union rules and all."

"Christ, I've missed you…" Luke breathes, bringing his mouth swiftly back to mine.

Let's hope our sentries stayed by the doors… I think briefly, tugging down my black lacy panties and bracing myself against the brick wall. It's the last coherent thought I have before I feel Luke's throbbing cock pressed against my slick sex. I bury my head against his shoulder as he drives up into me, my ecstatic cries muffled by the fine Italian wool of his suit.

How's *that* for function and fashion?

"Well," I pant, pushing my hair out of my face as I tug my dress back into place, "That's my new favorite way of saying 'hello again'."

"In that case," Luke replies, shrugging back into his suit jacket, "I vote we say 'hello again' three times a day, every day, for the foreseeable future…"

"There's a foreseeable future for us then?" I ask, straightening up on my sky-high heels. We got so distracted by our much-needed makeup, that the question of our future flew straight out of my mind. I almost don't want to think of it, now. Out here, away from our friends and families, it's easy to imagine that Luke and I are the only people in the world. If only it were that easy.

"Is that still what you want?" Luke asks.

"Well, to be honest, I don't think any future between the two of us would be at all *foreseeable*," I reply, "We can't predict anything that's going to happen, or plan for what might go wrong."

"I know that," Luke cuts in, running his hands down my bare arms, "And I've hated the thought of that, Sophie. I hate the idea of not having control over what happens to us next. That's what I've been wrestling with these past few weeks."

"How about this," I say softly, "For tonight, let's leave off with trying to predict the future. Let's just say that what happens next is us having an amazing time, drinking all the free booze we like, and partying our faces off."

"I guess there'll be plenty of time for adult conversation in the morning," Luke laughs, laying his hands on my hips, "We can spend tonight indulging in all the other adult activity we want."

"Deal," I grin, giving Luke a swift, hard kiss.

We hear the door crack open behind us, letting a roar of music escape out into the otherwise quiet night. Unlocking our lips, we turn to see Maddie and Cash sticking their heads through the cracked door. They look every bit the smug big siblings they are—I half expect Cash to break into a round of "Luke and Sophie sitting in a tree…" But luckily, they manage to contain themselves. Mostly.

"Come on lovebirds," Maddie says, "ReImaged wants some group pictures of the Asphalt brand ambassadors. I promise you can keep making out the second we've got a few shots."

"I *guess* we can manage that," I grin, lacing my fingers through Luke's.

"Speak for yourself," he shoots back, squeezing my hand.

We set off after Cash and Maddie, heading back into the fray of the party. Pure elation courses through me as I savor the feel of Luke's hand in mine. It feels so good to be out in the open with him, before the eyes of our siblings, the party-goers, our friends.

"Oh my god…" I laugh, as we make our way across the dance floor.

"What is it?" Luke asks, cocking his head at me.

"I just realized…We were supposed to go out together for the first time that last night at the lake," I gush, "So that means, technically…"

"This is our first date," Luke completes my thought with a gruff laugh.

"Worth the wait?" I ask, looking around the wild party.

"Always," Luke murmurs, his eyes fixed on me.

Something tells me it isn't just this date he's talking about, either.

Chapter Fifteen

I spend the night lifted up by a rushing swell of euphoria. The music, the booze, and the feeling of Luke's arms around me entwine in a dizzying cocktail. I can feel the stress and anxiety of the past few weeks melting away with each new song, each touch of Luke's lips against mine. I set down my burdens, kick off my heels, and have more uninhibited, raunchy fun than I ever have before. This night was bound to be incredible or devastating, but I didn't know it was going to be one of the best of my life.

It's early morning before the party even begins to break up. Luke and I are still on the dance floor, trying to keep the day from breaking by sheer force of will. But I can't hold my exhaustion at bay much longer, and Luke knows it full well.

"Come on," he yells above the music, "Let's get you into bed."

"Five more minutes!" I shout back, though my every muscle aches for rest.

"I'll make it worth your while, I promise," Luke grins, running his hands over the rise of my ass.

"Well, I can't very well argue with that," I say, throwing an arm over his shoulders, as he leads me off the dance floor at long last.

The second we clear the dance floor, I feel my weary feet leave the ground. I cry out with startled delight as Luke scoops me up into his arms, easily bearing my weight as we take our leave. Out of the corner of my eye, I spot Maddie across the room, shaking her head with a smile as she watches us go.

"How very gentlemanly of you," I laugh, as Luke carries me across the hotel lobby and into a waiting elevator.

"I want to get you upstairs and out of that dress as quickly as possible," Luke murmurs back as the elevator doors slide together, "But if that's what you call gentlemanly..."

"That's what I call fucking perfect," I breathe, kissing along Luke's throat as he holds me close.

The second the elevator doors slide open, my exhaustion is seared away with raw, lusty energy. I take off like a shot down the hall, racing Luke toward the door of my suite. He sprints along behind me, both of our raucous voice echoing off the pristine walls. I open the door and bolt inside with Luke on my heels. The momentum of our chase carries us across the suite, straight into the bedroom. Luke's arms circle my waist, picking me up off the floor once more before throwing me down on the sprawling bed.

"You realize this is another first, right?" Luke growls, kneeling over me with his gleaming green eyes hard on my body.

"What?" I ask, letting my knees fall apart under his gaze.

"Fucking in an actual bed," he grins, shrugging out of his suit jacket and lifting his shirt up over his broad shoulders. "You know, rather than the bed of a pickup truck."

"I'm sure we'll get used to it," I laugh breathlessly, drinking in the sight of his perfect chest, his cut abs, and the insistent bulge in his fine slacks.

I reach up to release his throbbing member, but he pushes me back hard against the bed, pinning me beneath him.

"You just lay back," he growls, kissing along my throat.

"Whatever you say," I breathe, my back arching as that sweet, warm pressure starts to mount inside of me.

Luke reaches around my back, tugging down the zipper of my tight red dress. He all but peels the garment away from my body, groaning as he sees my black lace panties and strapless bra.

"You wore my favorites?" he grins, running a finger under the band of my panties.

"I was dressing…optimistically," I breathe, closing my eyes as he snaps open my bra and takes both breasts in his firm, capable hands.

He runs his tongue over my hard nipples, taking one then the other into his warm, hungry mouth. Working down my body, he caresses every bit of me he can reach— with everything at his disposal. I buck my hips, grinding against the rock hard length of his cock…But he's not done with me just yet.

I gasp as his teeth close around my panties, tugging them clear down my legs before tossing them aside. He straightens up, towering above me as he runs his eyes all along my stark naked body. Only now, with his eyes fast on mine, does he whip open the buckle of his belt, letting loose that gorgeous, throbbing member I've come to love and crave.

"Luke," I whisper, pulling myself onto my forearms, "Please…Let me take you in my mouth."

His eyes flash brilliantly as he runs a hand up along my torso, his fingers lingering just below my throat. Slowly, he presses me back against the bed one last time. He brings his hands to my knees, spreading me wide open as he lowers that eager, grinning mouth.

"You first," he growls.

The feeling of his warm breath against my wet, aching sex sends goosebumps trailing all across my trembling body. A low, rasping moan rises up in my throat as Luke runs his tongue along the length of my slit, parting my pink lips as he presses back against my thighs. I grab onto handfuls of white bedding, bracing myself as his tongue traces slow, firm circles around my clit. Hot, bracing pangs of pleasure shoot up through my body with each swivel and flick of his perfect tongue. I cry out as he closes his lips around that aching button, sucking gently. I can feel myself filling up with bliss—it's only a matter of time before I spill over.

"You still want to taste my cock?" he growls, his lips vibrating against my clit as he flicks those green eyes my way.

"God yes," I gasp.

With athletic agility, he swings his towering figure around on the massive bed, pulling me to kneeling above him. He grabs hold of my hips, drawing my throbbing pussy back to his mouth as he lies beneath me. And standing tall right before my eyes is that delicious, piercing length I've been craving. Bracing myself on quivering forearms, I bring my lips to Luke's cock, closing my mouth around his bulging tip. He groans beneath me, grabbing firm hold of my ass as he flicks his tongue against my clit. We buck against each other as I take more and more of his staggering manhood into my mouth, running my tongue along the smooth expanse. I can feel him everywhere—and it's bringing me to the very edge.

"Luke," I groan, working my hands up and down his raging cock, "You're gonna do me in…"

"That's the plan," he laughs raggedly, giving me a push forward onto my hands and knees.

I have to close my teeth around the nearest pillow to keep from screaming as he eats me out from behind, lavishing my sex with his perfect mouth. My delirious, disoriented body can't hold back for a second longer. With one last decisive, leveling pass from Luke, I come hard and fast. Pleasure surges along my every nerve, lighting up my body from the inside out. Luke savors every last drop of my desire, licking the taste of me from his full lips. The mere sight of that is nearly enough to make me come all over again.

"Luke," I gasp, rolling onto my back as my chest heaves, "That…That was…"

"I know," he growls, lowering his body to mine. My mouth falls open as I feel his pulsating cock pressing against that wet, aching place between my legs. "I hope you have late check out for this room. We're gonna be needing it for a few more hours."

It isn't until dawn that Luke and I finally collapse into bed, completely spent with the fervor of our fucking. He was right about one thing—makeup sex would be a terrible thing to waste. I fall into a deep, dreamless sleep with my back pressed up against Luke's firm chest. His strong arms wrapped around me are dream enough, in my book.

The smell of rich, dark coffee draws me up out of my deep slumber hours later. Prying my eyes open, I glance at the bedside clock—it's already 10 a.m. Rolling over, I find that Luke has beaten me to the waking world. I glance through the open bedroom door and spot him in the kitchenette, pouring out two massive mugs of coffee.

Swinging my legs over the side of the bed, I stretch languorously. I grab Luke's white shirt from last night, sliding into it before padding across the suite toward him. He looks up as I sidle into the living room, grinning when he catches sight of my makeshift nightgown.

"It's not exactly as rugged as our last coffee date," he says, nodding toward the balcony, "But the view is still pretty decent, right?"

"I'd say," I reply, following my man out onto the patio overlooking the Seattle waterfront.

We settle down at a small table, sinking into our chairs and lifting our mugs in contemplative silence. Our bodies and minds are still numb with last night's lovemaking. The uninhibited peace makes me feel like I can speak freely, even about the hardest subjects. Which is convenient, since that's what we still haven't addressed during our blissful reunion.

"So," I sigh, swallowing a sip of coffee, "Once we leave this place today...Where are you headed next, Luke? I hear you've been drifting these past few weeks."

"It's true," he says, looking out over the horizon, "I've been on the move since we left the lake house. I just drove, mostly. Tried to clear my head. But I did make one last stop, back in my hometown. Just a couple days ago...I went back to speak with my father."

"You did?" I ask, whipping around to face Luke, "About...what?"

"About the things we were raised never to mention," Luke says, his jaw pulsing, "I told him, in no uncertain terms, that I'm not interested in being the heir to a man who doesn't respect me."

"Wow..." I breathe, "Luke, that must have been so hard."

"I would have thought so too," he replies, shaking his head, "Growing up, I was so in awe of my Dad. But as I've become a man, I can see him for what he really is. Scared. Alone. *Human.* That stunt he pulled at the lake house was the last straw. He doesn't have any power over me anymore, Sophie. And he certainly doesn't have any say in my future."

"Then...What's your next stop?" I ask softly.

"I guess that depends on you," he replies, swinging his gaze toward me. "And whether or not you'd mind if we stopped next in the same place."

"I wouldn't mind that at all," I tell him, a smile breaking across my face, "In fact, nothing would make me happier."

"I'm still not interested in being back at Sheridan," he says, "No more dwelling in the past. But I could be close by."

"Actually…" I tell him, "There's a chance that I may not be at Sheridan for too much longer either. There's a guest artist named Karen Krause who's got her eye on me for an acting apprenticeship. In New York."

"New York?" Luke echoes, tasting the words ponderously.

"Yeah," I tell him, "That could very well be my next stop."

"Well…I'd never think of it myself, but now that you mention it, New York seems like as good a next stop as any," Luke says, reaching for my hand.

"Really?" I ask softly, turning to face him, "You'd come across the country…Just to be with me?"

"If that's what you want," he replies, lacing his fingers through mine.

"It is," I tell him firmly. And the second I say it, I know that it's absolutely true.

"Guess I'd better start memorizing the subway map, huh?" Luke smiles, "And forming bizarrely intense opinions about bagels. But first, I think a shower is in order. Want to join?"

"In a second," I tell him, sinking back in my chair, "I have to remember how to walk, first."

Luke laughs, kissing me lightly on the forehead.

"This is going to be a great thing for us," he says decisively, "I can feel it."

I can feel it too, in every inch of my body. And all we had to do was let go of our stupid hang-ups about propriety, and what kind of love is "allowed". Luke and I are so much more than just a bundle of taboos. We're two people who care about each other. That's it.

Sighing happily, I carry my mug back into the kitchen for a refill. I can hear the running shower in the other room as I pour myself a second cup of smooth, black coffee. A chirp rings out from my purse, sitting on the kitchen counter. Sipping my fresh coffee, I pull out my cell. I perch on the counter, legs swinging lazily beneath me, to see who's just texted.

My stomach turns unpleasantly as I see that my mother has sent a group message to me, Maddie, and Anna. I've barely had more than a cursory word from her in three weeks. Once she was assured I was back at Sheridan, she carried on her own merry way. Maybe she's reaching out now to apologize to me and my sisters about the way she spoke to us that night at the lake? Maybe she's finally broken things off with John and come to her senses? That would be a lovely surprise.

Might as well get this over with, I think, pulling up the text. It's a picture message. No words, just a single photo. I cock my head at it, trying to discern its meaning. It looks like she forgot her phone was on and accidentally took an off-center selfie. The picture is framed around her frantically waving hand. The image is so blurry that I almost overlook the new, shining stone that rests on her ring finger.

My coffee mug shatters into a hundred pieces as I stare down at my phone, the blood draining from my slack-jawed face. I hear footsteps across the suite, muffled by the thundering sound of my own beating heart. Luke appears in the bedroom doorway, a white towel tied hastily around his waist. A look of concern twists his gorgeous features.

"What's the matter?" he asks urgently, "I heard a crash, and…Jesus, babe—you're white as a fucking ghost."

I try and make my mouth form the words he needs to hear, but no sound comes out. I'm gripping the edge of the counter, my knuckles going white. My breaths come high and shallow as my body refuses to process what's happened.

"Sophie, you're scaring me," Luke says, walking slowly toward me across the suite. "Talk to me. What's going on?"

I drag my eyes up to his, focusing with all my might on putting one word in front of another. I can scarcely believe the phrase I'm about to utter. It's surely too devastating to be true.

"They're engaged," I say, my voice barely audible. "Our parents are engaged."

Luke's body goes stock still as my words hit him hard from across the room. I watch his eyes flash with confusion, disbelief, and rage before they harden into stone once more. I know this look of his, by now. It's Luke, preparing himself for a battle.

Good thing, I think to myself in the deafening silence that unfolds all around us, *because I have the feeling we're in for the fight of our lives.*

***

The End

To Be Continued in Hawthorne Brothers, Book Three…

THANK YOU FOR READING

Please leave your honest review ☺

Also From Colleen Masters:

Stepbrother Bastard (Hawthorne Brothers Book One)
by Colleen Masters
Stepbrother Billionaire by Colleen Masters
Stepbrother Untouchable by Colleen Masters
Damaged In-Law by Colleen Masters

Faster Harder (Take Me... #1) by Colleen Masters
Faster Deeper (Take Me... #2) by Colleen Masters
Faster Longer (Take Me... #3) by Colleen Masters
Faster Hotter (Take Me...#4) by Colleen Masters
Faster Dirtier (Take Me...#5) (A Team Ferrelli Novel) by Colleen Masters

Made in the USA
San Bernardino, CA
07 March 2017